## THE CLUE OF THE HISSING SERPENT

Why is a wealthy sportsman so frightened by the serpent design on a mysterious balloon that he begs Frank and Joe Hardy to protect him? And who stole the ancient, life-size chess king which is to be presented to the winner of the world chess championship?

These questions and others equally as baffling in this exciting mystery seem to defy explanations.

On the ground and in the air Frank and Joe find themselves the targets of diabolical enemies. An odd clue that they discover leads them across the Pacific to Hong Kong. There the young detectives match wits with their adversaries. How they help the police smash an international criminal organization provides an electrifying climax to one of the most challenging cases the Hardy boys have ever tackled.

*To Frank's horror, both fell over!*

*The Hardy Boys Mystery Stories*®

# THE CLUE
# OF THE
# HISSING SERPENT

BY

FRANKLIN W. DIXON

GROSSET & DUNLAP
Publishers • New York
A member of The Putnam & Grosset Group

# CONTENTS

# CHAPTER I

## A Runaway Balloon

"Your father sounded desperate," Aunt Gertrude said, looking worried. "He wants you to meet him at four o'clock in the lobby of the Treat Hotel at Oak Knolls. Better hurry!"

Frank and Joe Hardy had just arrived home from a swim at the Bayport pool when their agitated aunt met them at the kitchen door. The telephone message seemed innocent enough, but Aunt Gertrude always feared the worst for her famous detective brother Fenton.

"Oh, yes," she continued, "he mentioned the word *Falcon*. What does that mean?"

"*Falcon!* Holy crow, Frank, let's go!" Joe urged excitedly.

The boys bolted out the door and into their car. Joe took the wheel and they sped off.

*Falcon* was a secret word used by the two young detectives and their father. It meant *dan-*

1

*ger ahead.* But what was the danger Fenton Hardy had foreseen in their meeting?

They mulled it over as they hit the speed limit and arrowed along the highway due west from Bayport. Mr. Hardy had not mentioned any new case. Hence, if there was danger, it had sprung up suddenly. Frank and Joe were worried.

Dark-haired Frank, who was eighteen, glanced at his watch. "Three o'clock. We should make it in time."

Joe, a blond seventeen-year-old, nodded. "I just hope it doesn't rain. Might slow traffic."

The sky, which had been bright and sunny during the morning, had turned ominously gray in the west and a chilly wind began to dissipate the late June heat.

"Looks like a storm is heading our way," Frank said. "And traffic's slowing already. But it can't be because of the weather. I wonder what happened."

"I guess there's been an accident." Joe craned his neck out the window for a better look. But all he could see was a line of cars moving at a snail's pace. Horns were honking impatiently. Then traffic stopped completely.

People began stepping out of their cars, and Joe did the same. Suddenly his eyes grew wide in amazement.

"Frank! I see the trouble!"

"What is it?"

"A balloon! Flying pretty low and coming closer to the road. Everybody's stopped to look at it."

Frank reached into the glove compartment and grabbed binoculars which the boys kept handy. He jumped out to scan the green-and-white striped balloon. Like a giant pendulum, it whipped dangerously back and forth.

"It must be caught in some kind of crazy wind current," Frank said. "Here, take a look, Joe."

Now the balloon was no more than a hundred yards away. Joe focused on the two passengers hanging desperately to the sides of the basket.

"What are they going to do?" he cried out. "Land on the highway?"

Suddenly the balloon veered to the right, coming to rest in a field beside the road not far from the Hardys.

Frank pulled the car over to the side. "Come on, Joe. Maybe we can be of some help."

A lot of other motorists had the same idea, and soon a huge crowd raced across the pasture to where the balloon was gradually deflating.

The boys were in the forefront and reached it first. The two balloonists were just climbing out. Frank's jaw dropped open in amazement as the younger one turned around to face them. It was none other than their staunch buddy Chet Morton!

"Hello, Frank. Hi, Joe," Chet said.

"What in the world are you doing here?" Joe demanded.

The chunky, freckle-faced youth squinted up at the collapsing balloon and remarked casually, "I'm taking lessons. Didn't want to tell you until I became a full-fledged balloonist."

His companion walked up to the group. "Oh, fellows," Chet said, "this is Mr. Albert Krassner. And these are my friends, Frank and Joe Hardy."

The man seemed to be about forty, with thinning black hair and a paunch. He had a broad, fleshy face, full lips, a wide nose and slightly droopy eyelids, which made him look half asleep. Yet there was a brisk alertness in his voice as he spoke.

"Glad to meet you." He extended a pudgy hand to the young detectives. "We really got into trouble. A sudden wind came up and we tried to land, but a faulty vent prevented us from getting down fast enough. We almost drifted onto the highway!"

"A faulty vent?" Joe asked.

Chet nodded. "You pull a cord to vent when you want to descend more rapidly than simply letting the balloon's air cool. The vent lets the air out—the longer you hold it open, the quicker. Ten feet above the ground you rip the top if the wind is high. It pulls off the circular panel and lets the hot air out in a rush."

*"Chet, what are you doing here?"*
Joe demanded.

"I see," Joe said. "But you have to be just above the spot where you want to land to do that."

"Right," Chet said.

Krassner went back and continued to deflate the balloon, answering questions of other onlookers. The Hardys took Chet aside and asked him about his new friend.

"He's a rich guy," Chet said. "An investment banker. Belongs to the Lone Tree Balloon Club near Oak Knolls."

"How'd you meet him?" Frank inquired.

"I used to hang around the club," Chet said. "Krassner took a liking to me and offered these lessons free."

"This could have been your last lesson, Chet!" Frank said. "You almost got killed!"

"And if you're such a buddy of ours, how come you didn't let us in on your new hobby?"

"Now don't get sore," said Chet. "I told you, I wanted to make it a surprise."

"It sure was," Frank said. Then he glanced at his watch. They had twenty minutes to reach their destination. "We've got to meet our dad at the Treat Hotel in Oak Knolls," he said. "See you later."

Traffic had started to unsnarl with the aid of two State Police men. As the boys hastened to their car, they saw a pickup truck drive across the field to retrieve the balloon. A small black sports car followed it.

"Probably Krassner's," Joe commented. "Looks like an Italian job."

The Hardys crept along for a while until they could pick up speed. Joe passed dozens of cars, but eased off on the gas when the needle exceeded the speed limit. "If we get a ticket, we'll never get there on time," he said.

Finally they reached the exit for the small town of Oak Knolls. By now it was ten minutes past four. When they drove into the parking lot, the clock on the tower in the town square stood at four-twenty.

The boys rushed into the hotel. "Any message for Frank and Joe Hardy?" Frank asked the desk clerk.

"No, nothing. Were you expecting to meet someone?"

"Yes." Frank looked worriedly about the lobby.

"Would you like accommodations?"

"No, thank you," Joe replied. He noticed a meeting room off to one side with the door open. The boys walked in. The place smelled smoky and cigarette butts lay in numerous ashtrays. Printed agendas were scattered on folding chairs and long tables.

On a dais at the far end of the room stood a blackboard. Chalked on it were numbers indicating that a business meeting had taken place.

"Maybe Dad attended," Frank mused. "It

couldn't have ended long ago." He took a closer look at the blackboard. In one corner something was printed in small letters. "Joe," he exclaimed, "it says *Mayday Room 211 Falcon!*"

"Dad's in trouble!" Joe said. "In Room 211!"

Suddenly both were startled by a voice behind them.

"The world's full of trouble!"

Frank and Joe whirled to confront Albert Krassner.

"W-what are you doing here?" Joe asked.

Krassner smiled blandly. "Chet told me where I could find you. He also told me you're the famous Hardy detectives."

"We're not famous," Frank said. "But our father is."

Actually, Frank and Joe had become as famous as Fenton Hardy, who had retired from the New York Police Department to set up his own private practice. Starting with a mystery called *The Tower Treasure,* the Hardy boys had solved many baffling cases themselves. Their previous one was known as *The Shattered Helmet.*

Joe said, "Mr. Krassner, if you want us to join your balloon club, we can't talk about it now."

"No, no. It's not that. I want you to help me!"

"How?" Frank asked.

Suddenly Krassner's face contorted with pain. He grabbed Joe by the shoulders. Before the boy could move, both landed on the floor with a thud.

## CHAPTER II

## *A Custom-made Rocket*

JOE pushed the man away and sprang to his feet, but Krassner did not move.

"He's out cold," Frank said. "Must have had some kind of attack!"

The Hardys knew that ill people sometimes carry instructions on them in cases of emergency. Joe went through the man's pockets. "Here's a bottle," he said. "And a note wrapped around it!"

They read it quickly. If Krassner suffered a heart seizure he was to be given one tablet under his tongue.

Frank administered the medicine. Seconds later Krassner opened his eyes. The Hardys helped him up and to a comfortable position on a sofa.

Joe ran out to get a glass of water. When he returned, some color had come back into Krassner's pale, puffy face.

He spoke in a shaky voice. "Sorry to be such a nuisance, boys. Guess I had too much excitement for one day. And I'm sure glad you found my pills."

"Think nothing of it," Frank said. "Why don't you just rest here a while? We'll be right back."

Krassner nodded and the two walked out of the conference room. "This is all very strange," Frank whispered. "We'd better find Dad fast." They hurried through the lobby and up to the second floor.

In front of Room 211 they stopped and listened quietly. At first they heard nothing. Then there was a thump and a low moan.

"Let's break down the door," Joe said.

"Wait," Frank replied.

He tried the knob. It turned and he pushed the door wide open. Inside, midway between a bed and a dresser, lay Fenton Hardy. He was bound hand and foot and gagged. The boys rushed over and freed their father. Stiffly the detective sat up and rubbed the back of his head.

"I thought you'd never get here," he murmured.

"Sorry," Frank said. "We were delayed by a balloon."

"What?"

"We'll tell you later, Dad. Get up now. Easy."

As they helped Mr. Hardy to a nearby chair,

Joe noticed a piece of paper stuffed into his shirt pocket.

"What's this?" he asked.

"I don't know," Mr. Hardy replied.

Joe took it and read the message. "Dad, it says, 'Keep your mouth shut.'"

"Fat chance!" Frank exclaimed. "Dad's a pretty hard man to intimidate."

The detective smiled wryly and told his sons what had happened.

"It all started with a telephone call to Sam Radley," he began, referring to an operative who had often helped him in his investigations. "The caller wanted Sam to bug the home of Conrad Greene in Ocean Bluffs."

"The United States chess champion?" Frank asked.

"That's the one."

"But why?" Joe queried.

"The world championship is coming up soon," Mr. Hardy said. "It might have something to do with that. Anyway, when Sam told me about it, I went in his place to see his so-called client."

"And met with him downstairs," Frank concluded.

"Correct. When I arrived, there were two men in the room. Obviously there must have been a group of people who had just left. I don't know whether the two men had any connection with them or not. They told me their names were Smith and Jones."

"Sounds as phony as a three-dollar bill," Joe said. "What did they look like?"

"Smith was short, slender, with long pointed fingers. He had a slightly Mongolian look. The other fellow, Jones, was strictly Anglo-Saxon. Long face, typically English, I'd say. Narrow thrusting chin. Both were in their late thirties.

"What I wanted you boys for," Mr. Hardy went on, "was to tail these men."

"Don't worry. We'll find them if they're anywhere in this area," Frank assured him.

"Anyhow," Joe said, "you told them it was no go on the bugging deal."

"Right. Then they invited me to Room 211 to talk it over some more. I excused myself on the way out because I forgot my briefcase. That's when I put the message on the blackboard."

"Good thing you did," Frank said.

Mr. Hardy nodded. "When I entered Room 211, a third person conked me from behind."

"Do they still think you're Radley?" Joe asked.

"I don't know. In any case, this illegal wiretapping must be stopped. If Smith and Jones find some dishonest detective to put a tap on Greene's phone, it could lead to real trouble."

Mr. Hardy felt better now and they went downstairs. Krassner was not in the meeting room, so they questioned the clerk at the desk.

He said that 211 had been rented as a hospitality room for a sales meeting of Eco Incorporated. "I've never heard of that company," he told them. "But one of the salesmen mentioned Associated Jewelers. They're a house-to-house operation with headquarters in Bayport."

"Did you see the gentleman who came in after us?" Frank asked.

"Oh yes. He left a little while ago."

The Hardys thanked the man and went outside. Frank and Joe explained about the delay on the highway and how Krassner had suffered a heart seizure.

"He sounds like an odd character," Mr. Hardy said. "Wanted help and didn't tell you why."

"Maybe he changed his mind," Frank said. "What now, Dad?"

It was decided that Frank and Joe would investigate the assault, because Mr. Hardy was occupied with a case involving Hong Kong custom tailors.

"The Association of Menswear Retailers wants me to track down this gyp operation," the detective said. "About half a dozen men are involved. They take orders for custom-made suits from Hong Kong, request a fat down payment, and disappear. It shouldn't take too long to crack it. Crooks like this usually aren't too bright."

Mr. Hardy drove out of the parking lot and the boys followed in their car. At home, Mrs. Hardy met her three men, as she called them, and asked, "What's this big mystery Gertrude was telling me about?"

Frank gave her the gist of what had happened and added, "Don't worry, Mother. Things are under control."

Mr. Hardy made a few phone calls, then said to his sons, "Eco Incorporated and Associated Jewelers are not listed in any trade register I can get hold of, but Associated Jewelers are in the phone book. I think Eco was just a phony cover for that company. I suggest you check it out."

"Will do," Frank said.

"I also called Conrad Greene's home to warn him about the wiretap, but no one answered."

"We'll have to try again," Frank said. "Let me see if I can get in touch with Chet to quiz him about Krassner."

Chet was home and took Frank's call. "Boy, Krassner was full of praise for you," he reported. "I just saw him a little while ago. Said you helped him when he had an attack."

"Do you have any idea what he wanted to talk to us about?" Frank asked.

"No. But why don't you drop by the balloon club tomorrow and ask him? He usually comes over early. Besides, I want to show you the setup."

"We'll be there."

Right after breakfast the next morning the Hardys started out for the club. Near Oak Knolls they turned off the highway at a sign announcing *Lone Tree Balloon Club*. A narrow lane led through the woods and to an open meadow. Off to one side was a frame structure no larger than a two-car garage. A single, large oak tree stood next to it.

Out in the field Chet Morton and another youth were busy unfolding the envelope of a red-striped balloon. Joe parked beside the clubhouse and the Hardys walked up to their friend.

"Hi, guys," Chet greeted. "I'd like you to meet Ken Flippen. Just call him Fearless. That's his nickname."

Frank and Joe shook hands with a slightly built boy of sixteen. A shock of black hair hung over his eyes and he tossed his head occasionally.

"Sure glad to meet you," Fearless said with a friendly grin. "Chet's clued me in on your detective work. Says you're on another important case. That must be exciting!"

Frank gave Chet a slit-eyed look. "What have you been telling people?"

"Can't I brag about my friends—a little?"

"Very little," Joe said, and turned to Fearless. "Don't believe everything this big panda tells you. By the way, what are you fearless about?"

"Aw, nothing."

"I know," Chet said. "When he was a kid, he hung onto a rope and got pulled into the air by a balloon. Hung on for ten minutes until it came down."

Fearless looked embarrassed, and Frank said, "There you go again, bragging about your friends!"

They all laughed and Chet said, "Fearless knows a lot about balloons. His father and two other men own this one. We're practicing inflation."

Fearless was pleased to tell the Hardys about his balloon. It had a two-man aluminum gondola or basket, and was lifted by hot air. Two propane gas tanks lay on the floor of the basket, and from each a stainless-steel tube led to a multiple pilot-light structure mounted on a metal framework above the gondola.

"When the pilot pulls this cord," Fearless said, "the blast valve releases propane which is ignited by the pilot light." He demonstrated, and a roaring blast of flame shot upward.

"This goes into the open mouth of the balloon," the boy went on, "keeping the air inside hot, or heating it more if it's cooled."

"Hey, that's keen!" Joe said. "You can carry your own hot-air furnace with you."

"Right. This balloon is made of flame-resistant nylon. If by accident the flame melts a hole in the fabric, it will not burn the balloon up."

Chet and Fearless proceeded to shoot hot air into the huge bag, and Chet said, "If you want to descend gradually, you don't shoot any more air in and the balloon will come down."

"There sure is a lot to know about ballooning," Frank said. "Chet, when will you get your pilot's license?"

"Maybe in a month," Chet said proudly.

Joe changed the subject. "Where's Krassner?"

"He didn't show up." Chet said. "That's unusual. I expected him early this morning. But maybe he doesn't feel too well. Why don't you wait a while?"

Frank shook his head. "No, we have some work to do. We'll catch up with him later."

"So long, Fearless," Joe said.

"Come back for a ride someday!"

"We will."

The Hardys went to their car, looking back once toward the balloon which was now partially inflated.

"Chet sure does latch on to some good hobbies," Frank said as they drove back to Bayport to investigate Associated Jewelers.

Their office was near the waterfront, and turned out to be a relatively new one-story building. Across the street stood an ancient three-floor wreck of a house bearing a sign: *Danger. Building Condemned.*

The boys parked and entered the jewelry company. In an anteroom were three chairs and a writing table. The door at the far end opened and a woman appeared.

"Are you answering our ad?" she asked.

Frank hesitated, "Why—er—"

"Then come right in. Mr. Jervis will talk to you."

The inner office contained four filing cabinets, a number of chairs, and a cluttered desk. Behind it sat a pale, thin man wearing thick-lensed glasses. A nameplate on the desk read: *Reginald Jervis*.

"Have a seat," he said with an ingratiating smile. "You're rather young, but we could use two men right now. What is your experience in door-to-door sales?"

Before either had a chance to reply, Jervis went on, "We have a fine line of jewelry, and if you succeed in selling it, we have another most attractive offer."

Finally Frank interrupted. "We don't want a job, Mr. Jervis."

"What? Then why are you here?"

"To ask some questions."

"About what?"

"About Smith and Jones. Who are they?"

"Never heard of them!" Jervis snapped.

"And you've never heard of Eco Incorporated, either, I suppose," Joe put in.

Jervis rose from his chair and pointed a finger at the door. "Get out!" he said.

"So you don't know Smith and Jones?" Frank said coolly. "Well, there are other ways to find out about them."

The boy's calm demeanor infuriated Jervis. "I said get out!" he yelled. "Or I'll throw you out myself!"

# CHAPTER III

## *Tricky Surveillance*

THE man pushed back his chair and took a step toward Frank and Joe.

"You don't have to get physical," Frank said. "We'll go."

Back in their car, Joe said, "We sure touched a sensitive nerve. Something fishy's going on at Associated Jewelers."

Frank nodded. "Jervis was really on edge. Now I'm sure Smith and Jones are connected with that outfit."

Joe suggested they visit the Bayport Better Business Bureau. "Maybe they can shed some light on Jervis's company."

The Hardys drove along the waterfront, past a number of Chinese-operated shops known as Little Chinatown. They stopped at a hamburger place for a quick snack, then proceeded to Main

Street, where the Better Business Bureau was located.

They were cordially received by the woman in charge of consumer protection. In answer to Frank's question, she replied that she had heard of Associated Jewelers. The Bureau had received numerous complaints of high-pressure salesmanship and shoddy merchandise.

"The company is on our list," the woman said. "So far, we haven't enough solid evidence against them to warrant a lawsuit."

"Has the public been warned?" Frank asked.

"There was a report in the newspaper," the woman replied. "But I'm sure that many people did not see it."

When the boys returned home they found that Mr. Hardy, in response to a tip from Police Chief Collig, had gone off to question several persons who had been cheated by the jewelry peddlers.

"He'll be home later," Mrs. Hardy said.

"I wish we could watch one of their salesmen in action," Frank said.

"Perhaps you can," Aunt Gertrude spoke up. "But for goodness sake, be careful. If they cheat people, there's no telling what else they're capable of."

Her nephews looked perplexed. "What are you talking about?" Joe asked.

"Mrs. Snyder," Aunt Gertrude said.

"Well, what about her?"

"Mrs. Snyder—you know, the one who lives on Lincoln Street—has arranged for an Associated Jewelers representative to come to her house. I just spoke to her a few minutes ago. Your father had already left. She told me a very nice man phoned her and offered free earrings for letting him show their products."

"When will he call?" Joe asked.

"I don't know exactly when You'll have to ask her."

"Gee, thanks, Aunty," Frank said. "This may be a big help in our case."

Just then the telephone rang. Frank answered. It was Krassner, inviting the boys to his home in a suburb of Bayport that evening.

"We'll be there," Frank said. "How about eight-thirty?"

"Roger. See you then."

"This sure is a big day for us," Joe said. "Come on, Frank. We've got a lot to do."

The boys had just stepped out of the house for the short walk to Mrs. Snyder's home when Biff Hooper came along with his hound dog, Sherlock. Biff was a tall, athletic high school pal of the boys.

"Hi, Biff," Frank said. "Is Sherlock taking you for a stroll?"

"Something like that," Biff replied with a friendly grin. "Matter of fact, I dropped by to ask you how about some tennis after supper tonight? I've got Tony Prito lined up for doubles."

"Sorry," Joe said. "We're busy."

"Official business?"

"Yes. We're interviewing one of Chet's friends. He may have a case for us."

"You mean Krassner, the balloon guy?"

"How'd you know that?" Frank asked in surprise.

"Chet was in town at noon. He keeps me posted on your doings."

Frank laughed. "Good old Chet. He's a balloon buff now."

"It's a good sport," Joe said. "I'm getting interested myself."

"Where you guys going?" Biff asked.

Frank told him.

"I'll walk you over," Biff offered as Sherlock strained at the leash.

The trio turned a corner and proceeded along the block to the fifth house on the right. On the front steps sat a huge, tawny cat. Sherlock lunged, nearly pulling the leash from Biff's hand.

"Hold it, Sherlock!"

The hound let out a mournful bay and the cat raced up a mimosa tree on the front lawn. The commotion brought an elderly couple to the porch. The man looked over the top of his eyeglasses.

"Get that hound out of here!" he ordered. "He's scaring Princess!"

"All right. No harm meant," Biff said politely. "So long, fellows. See you later."

As he left, Frank addressed the couple. "You're the Snyders, aren't you?"

The woman nodded with a prim smile.

"We're Gertrude Hardy's nephews Frank and Joe. May we talk to you a minute?"

"Of course."

Mrs. Snyder preceded the boys into the house while her husband went to retrieve Princess from the tree.

"You see, we love cats," the woman said. "Not that we don't like dogs, too, mind you."

It was then that the boys realized that there were cats all over the house. They seemed to blend into the furniture. Frank counted six in the living room.

"Please be seated," Mrs. Snyder said. "But be careful of our pets."

One of them jumped off the sofa where Frank and Joe were sitting. At the same time Mr. Snyder entered, carrying Princess. He dropped down in an overstuffed chair and stroked the animal in his lap.

"We're sorry about the dog," Frank said, knowing that it was the wrong time to ask for a favor.

"Don't worry about it. Tell us what we can do for you," Mrs. Snyder said.

"We understand you're expecting a visit from an Associated Jewelers salesman," Frank began.

"Yes, he's coming tomorrow."

"Well, there have been complaints about this company. High-pressure salesmanship and shoddy merchandise. It might have something to do with a case we're investigating, and we'd like to listen to what this man has to say to you."

At that moment he felt a terrible tickle in his nose and let out a resounding sneeze. "Excuse me, please."

Mr. Snyder nodded. "How are you planning to listen in?"

"We could conceal ourselves somewhere."

"Goodness! Wouldn't that be dangerous?" Mrs. Snyder asked.

"I doubt it," Frank said. "Anyway, we'd be here to protect you."

"I don't like it," Mr. Snyder said.

"Don't be grumpy," his wife intervened. "What would Gertrude think if we turned her nephews down?"

"Then may we come?" Frank asked hopefully.

"Certainly. The salesman is due at two. Why don't you stop by at one-thirty?"

Mr. Snyder looked none too pleased but did not object. The boys expressed their thanks and left.

At home, Frank and Joe praised Aunt Gertrude for her aid. "Did you know the Snyders have a houseful of cats?" Joe asked as the family sat down to dinner.

"Oh yes. One named Princess Golden Girl of Bayport is a champion."

When the meal was over, the boys set out for Krassner's home. It was located in a wooded area about twenty miles out of town.

The sun was setting as they neared the property. Suddenly they heard a strange hissing noise.

Frank slowed down. It was not from the car, but seemed to come from overhead. Both looked up in amazement to see a weird balloon. Hot air was gently shooting into the envelope with a sound like auto tires on a wet pavement.

"Look at those crazy colors!" Joe exclaimed as the craft drifted over the woodland. It was mottled in shades of green, blue, and yellow, and its central decoration was an evil-looking, twisting serpent of the same hues.

"Someone has an artistic touch," Frank said admiringly. "Let's follow it to see where it lands. It was flying pretty low."

"Okay. We have half an hour to spare, anyway."

They turned around and a hundred yards farther on found a narrow lane leading into the deep woods.

Overhanging branches brushed past the car as it probed deeper into the forest along the rutted trail. The slow going was maddening. But finally they reached a clearing.

Off to one side was a tumble-down barn, and

beside it a stark blackened chimney—all that remained of a burned-out farmhouse.

"Look," Frank said. "There's the balloon. And their pickup truck got here ahead of us."

They could see why. A good blacktop road was no more than a hundred yards away on the opposite side of the clearing.

Frank and Joe parked the car and trotted toward the barn. Perhaps the serpent balloonists were from the Lone Tree Club.

Behind the old building the deflated envelope was being packed up. Three men worked with great rapidity, and the balloon and gondola were loaded onto the truck. The men jumped in.

"Hey, wait a second!" Frank called out as he and Joe ran forward.

The truck started up and the Hardys hailed it again. But instead of slowing down, the driver accelerated. Frank and Joe moved to the side of a gully, because it was coming right at them!

"Holy crow!" Joe exclaimed. "They're trying to run us down!"

"Jump!" Frank cried out.

# CHAPTER IV

## *A Hissing Blast*

DIVING headlong, Frank and Joe cleared the side of the road and landed in a bramble patch as the truck sped by.

Joe rose painfully from the thorny foliage and Frank followed him, pulling thorns from his hair and clothing.

"Did you get the license number by any chance, Joe?"

"Oh, sure, I jotted it down while flying through the air!" he quipped. "Frank, do you think those guys have something to hide or are they just nasty?"

"I'd say both."

They brushed the weeds from their disheveled clothes and returned to their car.

"It must have taken months to decorate that balloon," Frank said.

"Right. Maybe they're entering a contest for

the most artistic design. Anyway, whoever was driving deserves an artistic punch in the nose."

Joe got into the driver's seat while Frank slipped in beside him.

"Ow!"

"What's the matter?" Joe asked.

"I didn't get all those confounded thorns out of my britches!"

They went back by the same route and regained the main road leading toward Krassner's home.

"I guess this is it," Joe said finally.

Dusk had settled now and the lights from their car illuminated a bronze plaque set in a huge boulder announcing the residence of Albert Krassner. A pebbled driveway traversed an acre of lawn extending like a green velvet collar around a sumptuous gray stone mansion.

"I'll say he's rich," Frank commented. "This place must be worth a small fortune."

As the car approached, an ornamental carriage lamp was turned on, casting a pleasant yellow light over a broad band of marble stairs leading to the front door.

Joe parked and they mounted the steps. Frank pushed a button set in the masonry beside the glass-and-wrought-iron door. When chimes sounded inside, a maid in a dark dress and starched white apron answered.

"You're the Hardy boys?"

"Yes, we are," Frank replied.

"Wait a moment, please. I'll see if Mr. Krassner is ready to receive you." She led them into a center hall, then mounted a broad stairway.

Frank and Joe looked around. Suddenly Joe whispered, "Frank! Come over here!"

On a table near the door was an Oriental vase. Frank moved closer. "The serpent design! It's almost like the one on that balloon!"

"Very similar."

Then something else caught Frank's eye. He went to examine a beautiful trophy cup. "Here's something interesting, Joe. Mr. Krassner is a chess champion!"

The inscription stated that the cup had been awarded for the regional chess title.

Just then the maid came down. "Mr. Krassner will see you now," she said.

She led the boys upstairs and ushered them into the largest bedroom they had ever seen. One side was completely lined with mirrors, reflecting the beautifully appointed interior. At the far side was an immense canopied bed and on it, propped up with large pillows, lay Albert Krassner. He beckoned Frank and Joe to his side.

"First of all," he said, "I want to thank you for helping me when I had that seizure."

"Are you better now?" asked Frank.

"Oh yes. I just wanted to take it easy for a couple of days. The old ticker gives me trouble now and then, but I can afford to have the best doctors."

"You are fortunate," Joe said.

"In that respect, yes. But money isn't everything. Learn that while you're young."

"That's the way we feel, sir," Frank said. "Personally, we prefer mysteries and adventures."

"That's what I wanted to talk to you about," Krassner said. "What's happening to me is a frightful, dark mystery. I need your help!"

Frank tried to ease Krassner's obvious tension and chuckled. "Speaking of frightful things, Mr. Krassner, we sure had an odd experience on the way over here."

"That's right," Joe added. "A crazy-looking balloon with a fantastic snake design flew over our heads like a hissing serpent."

"What? You saw it, too?" Krassner's face turned ghastly white against the pillow.

"Are you having another attack?" Frank asked, worried.

The man did not reply. Instead he pressed a small buzzer half concealed beneath the sheet and the maid appeared like a genie.

"Please see the boys out," Krassner murmured. 'I don't think I can take any more conversation tonight."

"I'm sorry if we upset you, sir," Joe said.

"No, no. It wasn't you. See you later."

The man waved a pudgy hand and the Hardys

were escorted to the front door. When it clicked shut behind them, they were silent for a moment.

Then Joe said, "I don't get it. Every time he wants to tell us what bothers him, he becomes so upset that he can't."

"He must have seen that balloon, too, and for some reason it scared the wits out of him. I wonder why," Frank mused.

"By the way, is he married? Did Chet ever mention it?"

"No. All he said is that Krassner's rich. And he wasn't kidding."

A crescent moon hung low in the dark sky as the Hardys went to their car. Joe drove to the main road and they hummed along toward Bayport. Suddenly Frank said, "There's that noise again!"

Joe took his foot off the accelerator and listened. They glanced up, but could see no balloon. The sound was coming from the back of their car!

Joe stopped quickly and they hopped out. "Look," Frank said, pointing to the tail pipe. Fire was shooting from it, accompanied by a hissing sound.

"Turn the engine off, Joe!"

But before Joe could move—*blam!* An explosion rocked the car and pieces of metal clattered to the roadway.

"What the dickens happened?" Joe blurted out.

"Get the flashlight and you'll see," Frank said.

They slid underneath the car and assessed the damage. The blast had ripped open the tail pipe, muffler, and resonator.

"They're blown apart," Frank said. "Somebody put a charge into the tail pipe!"

The boys picked up some of the metal debris and tossed it into the trunk.

"Who could have done it?" Joe asked. "Do you suppose Krassner was involved?"

"It's possible," Frank said. "Or maybe Jervis or his buddies were following us."

"How about the serpent balloon people? They didn't seem too fond of us, either."

"Well," Frank said, "speculation will get us nowhere right now. Let's see if this heap will go."

The engine started up, but the racket it made was fierce.

"It sounds like a machine gun," Joe quipped. "Hop in, Frank. The sooner we get home the better."

The Hardys drove on through the night, hoping to reach Bayport without further incident. Going through the village of Allendale, Joe slowed down in an effort to mute the exhaust.

"Hope we don't wake up everybody," he said as the car picked up speed once more.

Two miles farther on, a siren sounded behind them. Joe glanced into the rear-view mirror to see the revolving roof light of a police car.

"Frank, here comes trouble." He pulled to the side of the road, stopped, and got out.

An officer, hardly older than the Hardys, emerged from the squad car.

Frank and Joe walked up to him. "Is there something wrong, Officer?" Frank asked.

The policeman looked grim. "What were you trying to do?" he said. "Wake up the whole town? You drove through it like gangbusters."

"Oh," Frank said, "we're sorry about the noise. Had trouble with the muffler. In fact, it blew apart. We're heading for Bayport for repairs."

"Don't you know it's against the law, riding without a muffler?"

"We know," Joe said. "But the accident happened only a little while ago. We'll stop at the next gas station."

"They're all closed," the policeman said.

"Well, what do you want us to do?"

"I'm taking you to headquarters."

"Officer," Frank said, "we're not lying to you. The muffler blew apart just down the road!"

"Where's your driver's license?"

Joe handed it to him and the policeman studied it. "Hardy," he said. "The name sounds familiar."

"Our father is Fenton Hardy, the detective," Frank explained.

"That cuts no ice with me. You think that entitles you to privileges?"

"We don't want any privileges. Just give us a break so we can get this muffler fixed."

"Tell it to the magistrate," came the unyielding reply. "And now get in that bomb and follow me!"

Disgusted, the boys returned to their car and drove after the policeman to Allendale. He pulled up in front of an old house which had been converted into headquarters.

Inside, a small light illuminated the sparse office. The officer motioned for the Hardys to sit down, then made a phone call. Ten minutes later an elderly man arrived.

He was wearing pajamas under a light coat and looked suspiciously at Frank and Joe. "What's up?" he demanded.

"The charge is disturbing the peace while driving without a muffler," the officer said. To the Hardys he explained, "This is the magistrate."

Without listening to the boys' side of the story, the man declared, "Fine is twenty-five dollars."

"But we don't have that much with us," Frank said.

"Then we'll have to lock you up. Besides, you can't drive that car. It's got to be towed away!"

# CHAPTER V

## Cat Trap

JOE was visibly frustrated. He started to reply, but Frank realized that saying the wrong thing would make matters even worse.

"Cool it," he whispered to his brother. Then he turned to the magistrate. "Don't you think this is a bit much, sir? We haven't got the money to pay the fine and on top of that we can't even drive the car. What do you suggest we do?"

"That's your problem," the judge replied with a curt wave of the hand. "The law's the law. You stay here till that fine is paid." With that he walked out the door.

"Being such a small town," the officer said, "we just have one cell. Get the money up or in you go!"

"May I use the telephone?" Frank asked.

"Sure. Calling your lawyer?" the policeman asked.

"Of course not. I'm going to talk to my father."

Aunt Gertrude answered, and to Frank's dismay told him that Mr. Hardy was not home yet. But she detected the frustration in her nephew's tense question.

"Are you in trouble?" she asked, then answered her own question, "Yes, you're in trouble. I can tell by your voice. Laura, get on the extension. The boys are in trouble!"

Frank heard a click, then his mother said, "What's the matter, Frank?"

"We've been arrested."

Both women gasped. "What for?" Mrs. Hardy asked.

"The muffler broke. The car makes an awful racket and the law says you can't drive like that."

Frank explained where they were and his mother said, "That's a shame. It would only be a short drive home."

"Makes no difference in this place," Frank said quietly. "We need twenty-five dollars to pay the fine and we'll have to get the car towed."

Joe gave his brother a nudge. "Ask Mother to get in touch with Tony Prito. He can pick up the money and rescue us with his father's truck."

Frank nodded and passed on the information.

"I'll call Tony right away," Mrs. Hardy promised.

The policeman allowed the boys to sit in the office while they were waiting. An hour later a

half-ton pickup stopped in front of the building.
Out stepped Tony Prito, a handsome boy with
black curly hair, whose father owned a construc-
tion company.

"Are we glad to see you!" Joe greeted him.
"This hasn't been our day!"

"Always call Prito for immediate service,"
Tony quipped. He handed Frank the money to
pay the fine. Then the boys went out, put a tow-
line from the truck to the car, and drove back to
Bayport.

When they arrived at the Hardy house, Tony
said, "Biff and I will help you make the repairs
tomorrow, okay?"

"Thanks," Joe said. "We'll go down to the auto
store first thing in the morning and get the parts."

Mr. Hardy had come home half an hour earlier
and listened while his sons told about the weird
balloon, the strange visit to Krassner, and the explosive charge in their tail pipe.

"Krassner sounds like a man in trouble," Mr.
Hardy said. "Did he give any inkling of what's
bothering him?"

"Nothing, Dad," Frank replied.

"Well, boys, it's after midnight. Let's hit the
sack and talk more about this tomorrow."

The next morning after breakfast Frank and
Joe went to an auto store and returned with the
necessary parts to repair their car.

Biff and Tony were already waiting with a couple of heavy-duty jacks, and soon they were busy at work underneath the automobile.

At lunchtime Mrs. Hardy brought out sandwiches. The boys got cleaned up and took a half-hour break, then continued with their installation. By one o'clock they had still not finished.

Joe said, "Frank, why don't you go over to the Snyders', and I'll stay here until the job's done?"

"Good idea," Frank agreed. He washed the grease from his hands, took a shower, and put on clean clothes. He entered the Snyders' house shortly before the salesman was scheduled to arrive.

"I found a good place for you to hide," Mrs. Snyder said. "Near the entrance of the living room is a closet with sliding doors. Get in there and peek out when the man comes."

"Thank you," Frank said. "That's just perfect."

The bell rang. "Get inside, hurry!" the woman said and went to answer it.

Frank hid in the closet and closed the doors, leaving only a small crack through which he could observe the living room.

Mrs. Snyder walked in with a stocky man. He had a large black mustache and a beard, and introduced himself as Mr. Horgan.

Mrs. Snyder beckoned him to sit down on the

sofa. He did, putting a sample case on the floor.
Then he opened the bag and revealed a large se-
lection of costume jewelry.

"Here are your earrings, ma'am," he said. "A
present from Associated Jewelers."

Mrs. Snyder accepted the gift graciously and
put them on.

"They're lovely," Horgan said, beaming. "Now
look at these other things, ma'am."

The woman examined the baubles which Horgan showed her. She tried on a necklace, held
brooch after brooch to her dress to study the effect, and slipped several rings onto her fingers.

Horgan looked up nervously once in a while.
Then he stood up and walked to the window.

"Are you expecting someone?" Mrs. Snyder
asked.

"No, no. It's just not my nature to sit still."
Horgan smiled. "Now which of these beautiful
pieces of jewelry would you like to buy?"

At this point Frank became aware of something
he had not noticed before. He felt a slight movement in the darkness and reached out. The tail of
a cat gently brushed past his leg!

"Good grief!" Frank thought. "Another one.
They're even in the closet."

The animal wanted to get out and began
scratching on the door. Frank picked up the cat,
hoping to keep it quiet, while Horgan went on
with his sales spiel.

*"Get inside, hurry!"* Mrs. Snyder said.

He would give Mrs. Snyder a lovely brooch if she would allow a friend to fit Mr. Snyder for a Hong Kong custom-tailored suit.

"You see, ma'am, the cost of labor in Hong Kong is very cheap and the tailors are excellent. My friend can take your husband's measurements, airmail them to Hong Kong, and deliver the suit in about four weeks."

"I'll have to ask Ralph about it," Mrs. Snyder said. "Wait a moment. I'll be right back."

When she left the room, Horgan walked to the window again and looked out with a nervous expression.

Frank's mind whirled. "Associated Jewelers must have taken on a new line—Hong Kong suits," he thought. "I wonder if it's legitimate. Maybe it has something to do with that tailoring racket Dad's working on." He felt a tickle in his nose and suppressed a sneeze.

He still held the cat in his arms, but now it strained to get free, meowing loudly. Horgan cocked his head to listen.

Frank muffled another sneeze. Suddenly he knew why. The cat's fur! He must be allergic to it.

Horgan turned and stared at the closet. The cat, meanwhile, clawed Frank's arm and yowled. He had to sneeze again. His eyes began to water, and he felt as if he were choking. "It's no use," he thought. "I need air." He opened the doors, sneezing loudly, and the cat flew out, landing in the middle of the living room.

The effect on Horgan was electric. His eyes bulged wide and his jaw dropped open. When he realized he was being spied on, the salesman let out an oath and dashed out of the house!

## CHAPTER VI

## *A Risky Chance*

FRANK watched the man jump into his car and speed away as Mrs. Snyder came back into the living room.

"What happened?" she asked. "Why did Mr. Horgan run off like that? And he left his case!"

Frank quickly explained and showed Mrs. Snyder the scratches on his arm.

"Did Princess do that? Oh dear! I'll get some antiseptic." She returned a few minutes later and daubed Frank's arm.

"What are you going to do with that sample case?" she asked.

"Use it for evidence," Frank replied. "Maybe we can identify that salesman through his finger prints. I'm sure Horgan uses an alias."

Frank took out his handkerchief and clicked the case shut. "If he comes back for it, tell him it's being delivered to Associated Jewelers. And thanks for your help, Mrs. Snyder."

When he arrived home, the repair work on the car was done and Biff and Tony had left. Frank went up to their father's comfortable study, where he found the detective talking to Joe.

"Dad, tell Frank what you found out," Joe urged.

Mr. Hardy sat back in his swivel chair and smiled. "The Hong Kong tailoring racket I'm supposed to crack is tied in with various jewelry sales operations. When the jewelry business slacks off, they offer to have their customers measured for a suit.

"After they receive the down payment, the clothing is never delivered. By the time the customers catch on, the swindlers have skipped town."

"What are you grinning at?" Joe asked his brother.

"I found out the same thing."

"At the Snyders'?"

"Right. And here's the sample case of an Associated Jewelers salesman."

"That ought to be a real good clue," Mr. Hardy said. "You didn't disturb the fingerprints, I hope."

"No. I was careful about that," Frank replied.

Joe went for their fingerprint kit and set to

work dusting the black plastic covering of the sample case. Horgan had provided them with a neat set of prints of both his left and right hands.

"We'll take these down to headquarters. Maybe Chief Collig can find out whether Horgan really is who he says."

"What I don't understand," Frank said, "is why Smith and Jones, who are obviously connected with Associated Jewelers, wanted to bug Greene's phone. I mean, that's out of their line."

"We assumed that they worked for Jervis because he acted so strange when we mentioned their names," Joe said. "Maybe we were wrong."

"But they also wanted to meet Radley at the Treat Hotel, where Associated Jewelers had a sales meeting," Frank said. "It's just too much coincidence."

"And Krassner's an enigma, too," Mr. Hardy added. "You said he was a chess player himself. Maybe there's a connection between him and Greene."

Joe sighed. "And where do those crazy balloonists come in? And who blew up our tail pipe?"

"Questions and no answers," Frank said. "What do we do next?"

"Take the fingerprints to the police first thing in the morning," the detective said. "And keep Associated Jewelers under surveillance."

"There's a vacant building right across the

street," Joe said. "Maybe we could use that to spy on them."

"By the way, Dad, did you warn Conrad Greene about the bug?" Frank asked.

"I tried but no one's home yet."

Just then the doorbell rang. It was Chet. "I have some good news," he said brightly.

"No kidding," Frank said. "Did you get your balloonist's license?"

"No, not yet. But Mr. Krassner feels better and wants to see you."

"When and where?" Joe asked.

"Tomorrow afternoon at the clubhouse. Can you make it?"

"Sure. We'll be there."

The next morning the Hardys took the fingerprints to Chief Collig. He was a heavy-set, slow-talking man, who had cooperated with the Hardys on many cases.

When Frank and Joe told their story, he congratulated them on their detective work. "We'll take the sample case to Associated Jewelers to see Jervis's reaction," Frank said. "Is that okay with you, Chief?"

"Sure. Go ahead. If the prints tell us anything, I'll let you know."

When they arrived at Jervis's office, the receptionist told them that her boss was out.

"Well, we have something that belongs to him," Frank said. "When will he be back?"

"Wait a moment," she said and walked out of the room. A few seconds later she returned. "He's in now," she said.

The boys entered the office and laid the sample case on the man's desk. "We thought you'd like to have this back," Frank said. "It must be valuable."

Jervis opened the kit. "This doesn't belong to us," he said.

"Mr. Horgan, who used it, claimed to be a representative of Associated Jewelers," Joe said.

Jervis remained cool. "We have been bothered by impostors lately," he said. "Trying to use our good name."

"And you don't try to sell Hong Kong tailored suits, either?" Frank said.

Jervis's mouth twitched a little. "Of course not. And now, get lost. I'm busy!"

As the boys walked out they could hear him grab the telephone off the cradle.

"Somebody's going to catch it!" Joe said with a grin.

"*Tsk, tsk.* Poor old Horgan," Frank said in mock sympathy as they drove home.

During lunch Chief Collig phoned. "Horgan is an alias," he reported. "The man's real name is Gerard Henry. He has a long record of petty crime."

"I had a hunch he wasn't on the level," Frank said, and told about their visit to Jervis. "We'd like to stake out his place," he concluded.

"There's an old building across the street where we could set up some cameras."

"Just be careful," the chief warned. "The place is unsafe. Also, we flush out vagrants now and then. Mostly junkies. They stay there at night."

"We'll watch out," Frank promised. "Thanks for your help, Chief."

The boys told their father the latest news and that they were planning to set up surveillance equipment.

"We'd like to start right away," Frank said, "but we have an appointment with Krassner this afternoon."

"I can't pitch in, either," Mr. Hardy said. "I have a meeting. But maybe Sam Radley could help us out."

A telephone call brought the detective's sandy-haired operative to the Hardy home. He agreed to begin surveillance immediately.

Frank and Joe loaded film into a movie camera and a still camera with a telescopic lens. They also brought a two-way radio and a folding chair and drove off with Sam.

They parked on a street behind the old building and worked their way through an alley to the rear entrance.

"This place certainly is in bad shape," Sam commented as they entered a broken door leading to a flight of badly tilted stairs.

"It even smells rotten," Joe said, sniffing the musty odor of the interior.

They climbed to the third floor and saw no sign of habitation. Sam checked all the windows until he found a suitable spot. "How about right here?" he suggested.

The boys set up the cameras on tripods and focused clearly on the entrance to the Associated Jewelers office.

"If anyone goes in or leaves, take his picture," Frank said. "We'll join you later."

"Okay." Radley adjusted the folding chair and waved to the boys as they made their way downstairs and out the back.

When the young sleuths arrived at the balloon club, Krassner and Chet were already there.

"Frank, Joe I'm glad you came," Krassner greeted them.

"You're looking great today," Frank said.

"That's the way it is. These attacks knock me out for a couple of days, but I bounce right back."

"We thought that snake balloon got you upset," Joe said.

Krassner smiled. "Oh no. That was nothing."

Frank said, "We noticed a similarity in the balloon design and the serpent figure on your vase."

"You mean the one in the hall?"

"That's the one."

"Oh yes. Antique Chinese. They used that

pattern a lot. Well, Fearless is going to inflate his father's balloon. Chet, why don't you see if he needs help?"

"Sure thing," Chet replied, and hurried out to the grassy clearing.

Turning to the Hardys, Krassner said, "I want to talk to you alone about my problem. And I don't want to go to the police. Once the newspapers get wind of a thing like this, there's a lot of publicity, even notoriety. And in the investment business—well, you know how it is."

"Just what is the trouble?" Frank asked.

"My life has been threatened," Krassner said. "I'll be killed unless I hand over the Ruby King!"

# CHAPTER VII

## *Aerial Surprise*

"THE Ruby King? What's that?" Frank asked.

"A fabulous chess piece," Krassner replied. "A beautiful work of art made centuries ago in China. It is decorated with Burmese rubies and was part of a set made for an ancient warlord."

"Where are the other pieces?" Joe asked.

"Gone. Vanished in the mists of antiquity," Krassner said poetically. "That's one of the reasons why the Ruby King is so valuable."

"And you're in possession of it?" Frank queried.

"Yes. But it's not really mine." Krassner explained that he was part of a consortium of wealthy chess enthusiasts who had purchased it in China.

"We're going to present it to the winner of the world chess championship. Meanwhile, the prize is in my safe."

Frank and Joe knew about the match, which was to take place in Hong Kong the following month. It would pit the United States champion, Conrad Greene, against the Oriental title holder, a Korean named Chan Loo Duc.

Was there a connection between the valuable Ruby King and the intended wiretap on Greene's telephone? Obviously someone wanted the chess piece badly.

"Isn't your safe a rather vulnerable place?" Frank asked. "I think a bank vault would be better."

"My safe is very strong," Krassner replied. "Now I want you to keep our conversation in confidence. The whereabouts of the Ruby King is known only to a few people."

"Whoever threatened you must have found out," Joe said.

"That's what worries me. I want both of you to be on call in case of emergency."

Frank felt an uneasy suspicion about the man. Why would a rich banker ask the Hardys to shield him when he could well afford to hire an entire protection service? He put the question to Krassner.

"I'll tell you why," Krassner replied. "Life would be unbearable with an army of bodyguards. The press would be on my back with all kinds of speculations and innuendos." He stopped and smiled. "Besides, Chet Morton tells me you have never failed to carry out your assignments to the fullest satisfaction of your clients."

"You flatter us," Joe said with an embarrassed grin. "We'll do all we can to help you."

"But first," Frank added, "we'd like to see the Ruby King."

"Yes, I'll have you over the house soon. Here comes Chet."

The husky boy strode purposefully over to the three. "How about some ballooning today, Mr. Krassner?" he asked.

"That was my plan."

"Great. You can take Frank and Joe, and I'll go with Fearless."

"That'll be keen," Joe said.

"You've never been up before?" Krassner asked.

"Only in airplanes," Frank replied. Both Hardys were experienced pilots and often flew a plane which their father kept at Bayport Airport.

"I'm sure you'll like this kind of flying," Krassner said. "Come on. Let's get ready."

Everybody helped with the preparations. Krassner telephoned for two pickup trucks while the boys inflated the envelopes. People from the surrounding farms gathered to watch the spectacle of a twin ascension.

"They can hold the ground ropes for us," Fearless said. "It's a great sport."

Between bursts of hot air from the burners, the boys discussed ballooning. Chet proved to be a competent historian on the sport. He said two Frenchmen, the Montgolfier brothers, made the balloon used in the first recorded human flight over Paris. The year was 1783.

"Aeronauts have had plenty of adventures since then," Chet said. "Did you know that Napoleon used balloons to spy on the enemy? They were popular in the Civil War, too. And then there was a guy named Andrée who tried to fly over the North Pole in a giant balloon."

"Did he make it?" Joe asked.

Chet shook his head sadly. "I'm afraid not."

"All right, men," Krassner called out. "We're nearly ready." He and Fearless checked their radios and altimeters. The pyrometers, which measured the heat in the bags, were in working order. So were the variometers, needed to tell the rate of climb.

Just then the two pickup trucks arrived. The crowd cheered as the five stepped into the baskets. They held on tightly to the ground ropes until Fearless bellowed, "Hands off!"

Up went the two craft in perfect weather conditions. There was hardly any wind and a clear blue sky. The huge license numbers on the rounded sides stood out brightly in the late-afternoon sunshine.

Standing beside Krassner, Frank felt an exhilaration unlike anything he had experienced in an airplane. As the ground fell away beneath them in silence, the boy was engulfed in an unreal feeling of total peace.

Below, the waving spectators grew smaller, and the pickup trucks set off on the road, as a gentle fluff of wind sent the balloons on their way.

Krassner and the Hardys watched the other craft behind them as they drifted higher and higher. A farm slid past below them and three dogs looked up and barked furiously. Frank was surprised he could hear them so far off.

"Enjoying yourself?" Krassner asked. He picked up binoculars and scanned the countryside.

"I never had such a good time in my life!" Joe said enthusiastically. "Thanks a million for the ride."

"Don't mention it." Krassner's face looked serene. "Ballooning takes you away from all the world's troubles."

But the flight did not lull Frank's mind. It kept working to find the missing links in the puzzle. Was the Ruby King contraband—perhaps stolen in China? Was that the reason Krassner had shunned the police?

As they sailed on silently, the Hardys studied the uninhabited woodland carefully. It was not at all like the view from a fast-flying airplane. Suddenly Frank heard the radio crackle:

"Frank, this is Chet. Do you read me?"

"Roger. What a swell ride!"

"Listen. There's another balloon."

"Where?"

"At three o'clock."

Frank turned around. "I see it."

"Look close," Chet advised, and Frank asked Krassner for the glasses. He trained them on the third craft. *It was the serpent balloon!*

Frank told Krassner, and his face again showed tension and fear.

Chet's voice sounded once more. "Keep an eye on the snake. It's armed!"

Frank focused the binoculars on the other gondola. Three men were in it and one had a rifle. There was a muzzle flash, then a bullet whistled over them.

"They're firing at us!" Krassner screamed.

"Duck!" Joe ordered, "and let's land as fast as possible!"

Frank radioed to Chet, "We're descending. Better come with us."

"Roger."

Krassner had regained his composure, and Frank admired his airmanship. The man pulled open the vent and the craft sank rapidly. Three more shots sounded in the distance, but Krassner's fast-moving balloon made a difficult target. However, two slugs ripped through the balloon.

The wind freshened and the sinking balloon picked up speed. Frank saw that Krassner was heading for a small farm at the edge of the woods. There was a level, cleared area bordered on one side by a pond, on the other by an electric power line.

Fearless and Chet were close behind, but the serpent balloon made no attempt to follow them down. As their attackers flew out of sight, Frank talked to Chet again.

"Did you get a look at the snake's license number?"

"Affirmative. But Fearless says it's a phony. And listen to this. The snake has a little propeller, probably battery driven. That's how it caught up with us."

"The police should be notified."

"I've already done that," Chet said. "Called the pickup trucks and told them to phone the State Police."

"Good thinking. We're landing now. See you later."

Krassner maneuvered the craft toward the middle of the field while the farm children ran out of the house to witness the descent. The electric wires seemed a safe distance to their left and the pond far enough to the right.

"You're a great pilot, Mr. Krassner," Joe said tersely.

"We're not down yet— Oh, oh, trouble!"

An errant gust hit the balloon, carrying it toward the power lines. Frank and Joe were gripped by a sickening feeling as the metal wires loomed ominously closer.

"The blast valve!" Krassner shouted. "It's over your head, Joe. Pull it!"

Joe reached up and grasped the lever, sending hissing flame into the envelope. Nothing happened.

"It's not working!" Frank cried out.

"It will in time," Krassner said. "At least I hope so!"

Several seconds passed, then all at once the balloon lifted. The gondola cleared the power lines with two feet to spare!

Krassner looked limp and Frank let out a sigh of relief.

Joe shook his head. "We almost got fried!" he said.

The balloon dropped down once more and landed beside the farmhouse.

In their excitement the Hardys had paid no attention to how Fearless and Chet were faring. Now they jumped out of the basket, with Krassner on their heels, and ran to avoid the collapsing envelope.

Only then did they notice the other balloon. It was descending rapidly over the pond.

*Splash!*

Chet and Fearless hit the water like homecoming astronauts!

# CHAPTER VIII

## *A Tough Break*

FRANK and Joe raced toward the pond, followed by a farm boy and his two sisters dressed in Levis. When they reached the water's edge, Fearless was splashing toward shore.

"Where's Chet?" Frank yelled.

Fearless glanced back, reversed his course, and swam furiously to the spot where the basket had sunk. The Hardys dived in at the same time and with powerful crawl strokes reached it seconds later. They gulped in deep breaths of air and aimed for the bottom.

Meanwhile the three youngsters ran for their rowboat which was tied to a small dock.

"Jenny, Wendy," the boy shouted, "if we get the balloon out, maybe we can keep it!"

"Don't be silly, Kurt," the elder girl said as they pushed the boat into the pond. "Come on, Wendy, we'll row."

In the clear water, Frank and Joe saw Fearless trying to free Chet's foot which had become entangled in the coil of rope lashed to the side of the gondola. Frank helped give a final tug, and Chet, nearly unconscious, was whisked to the surface.

He was quickly towed ashore and pulled up onto the grass, where he lay gasping.

"You took in a lot of water," Frank said. "Just lie still for a while."

In the confusion of the rescue, no one had paid any attention to Krassner. Suddenly they heard a feeble call. "A pill! Give me a pill!"

Joe ran to the man, who was lying helpless on his back and quickly gave him the medicine. Minutes later Krassner sat up shakily. "Someone's out to get me!" he moaned. "My heart can't take this terror much longer!"

"Don't worry, Mr. Krassner," Joe said. "We'll get to the bottom of this whole thing yet."

While the farm children were busy retrieving the sunken gondola and the deflated envelope, the balloonists talked about their scary adventure. Joe was of the opinion that the serpent gang was only out to frighten Krassner.

"With a telescopic sight they couldn't have missed," he reasoned. "Besides, they didn't bother to pursue us any farther when we descended."

"You may be right," Frank said.

Krassner turned the situation into a feeble jest.

"Well, if they tried to scare me, they certainly succeeded."

"But why, Mr. Krassner?" Fearless asked. "What do these men have against you?"

Krassner avoided answering the question, and the boys busied themselves with the balloons. First they folded up Krassner's craft, then set about to help Jenny, Wendy, and Kurt drag the other one up onto the shore.

"I haven't seen your mom and dad," Joe said.

"They're in town with the truck," Kurt said. "Wow, wait till they hear what happened. Are finders keepers?" he added mischievously.

"Hey, this is no toy!" Fearless chuckled. "But for a reward, how would you like a ride some time next week?"

"Oh, that'd be great!" Wendy's eyes sparkled.

"Look, here come the State Police," Jenny declared.

Two squad cars drove right up to the pond, and a pair of uniformed officers plied the balloonists with questions about the mid-air assault. During the interrogation, the farm children said they had noticed the weird serpent balloon about four or five times in the past month.

But no one could shed any light on its owners, or why they had shot at Krassner. The man himself made no mention of the Ruby King.

A few minutes later the pickup trucks appeared and the equipment was loaded. It was dusk when they reached the balloon club, where the gear was stowed away.

"So long, everybody," Joe said as he and Frank went to their car.

"I'm going to your house first," Chet said. "I want to be in on the rap session with your dad."

"You ought to go home and hit the sack," Joe advised. "You've had quite a day."

"No, really, I feel fine now. I'll phone my folks so they won't worry."

Chet followed the Hardys to their house. When the two cars pulled into the driveway, Mrs. Hardy and Aunt Gertrude ran out to meet them.

"You had us worried to death!" Mrs. Hardy said. "We heard a radio report that several balloonists had an aerial war!"

"You were in it—yes you were!" Aunt Gertrude stared at them piercingly, then shook a skinny finger. "Now tell us all about it!"

"I guess the State Police released the news," Frank said and reported what happened. "Where's Dad?" he added.

"Out looking for you," Laura Hardy replied.

"Did he talk to Sam over the radio before he left?"

"Yes. It seems Sam had some success in his surveillance."

"Let's get in touch with him right away," Joe said.

They used the set in their car and called

Radley. There was no reply. They tried again. Nothing!

"Either his set's out of order or something's happened," Frank declared.

Chet, meanwhile, had wandered into the house looking for food. Aunt Gertrude, who had anticipated their need for sustenance, had ham sandwiches ready for them. Chet phoned home, then called out, "Come on, fellows. Let's eat!"

"Forget it," Joe replied. "Something might be wrong at our surveillance post. We're going over there right away."

"Wait for me!" Chet grabbed a fistful of sandwiches and wriggled into the back seat.

The three boys ate on the way. When they reached the street behind the old building, Frank turned off the lights and they crept cautiously toward the alley leading to the back entrance.

Armed with flashlights, which they used only sparingly, they ascended the crooked, creaking stairs. The rotting rooms smelled damp and unpleasant. All was quiet.

On the third floor Frank's light flashed into the room where Radley was stationed.

The boys gasped. Sam lay unconscious on the floor, a deep gash on the side of his head.

Chet said, "I think he's dead!"

"He's breathing," Frank assured his pal. As the Hardys administered first aid, Frank noticed that blood had congealed around the wound.

"Joe, this must have happened a while ago," he said and ripped off a shirttail. He tore it into strips and fashioned a bandage. As he applied it, Radley moaned and his eyelids fluttered.

"He's coming to," Joe said.

They helped the man gingerly to his feet and Frank said, "Chet, grab my flashlight and round up the equipment while we take Sam to the car."

"Will you be back?"

"Sure. You can't carry it all yourself."

Chet listened to their creaky footsteps fade away on the stairs. Then he shone the light around the room looking for the cameras.

"Holy crow!" he murmured. "I can't see them anywhere. They've probably been stolen."

He got down on his hands and knees and felt about the wooden floor until he came to an old door. It had been broken down and lay propped against the wall in one corner. Chet lifted it. Underneath was the still camera, its long lens sticking out like a telescope!

"Sam must have had enough time to hide it," he thought as he picked it up. Then he froze. Were those voices drifting up from below?

He did not move a muscle, hardly daring to breathe. Now he could hear voices distinctly. They were not Frank's and Joe's. There were quiet whispers, interspersed with oaths!

Then everything was silent for a while, until

footsteps sounded again. "The Hardys must be coming back!" Chet thought.

All at once angry shouts filled the old house, punctuated by scuffling and banging.

Chet grabbed the camera and raced downstairs. On the second floor landing he found Frank and Joe dazed and sprawled out on the dirty floor.

The Hardys pulled themselves to their feet slowly. "What a blitz!" Frank murmured, rubbing his head.

"How many of them?" Chet asked.

"Four dirty bums."

Joe grasped his jaw and moved it from side to side. "Nothing broken, I guess," he said. Then he felt in his pockets. "But my wallet's missing. And so's my watch!"

"Mine, too," Frank said. "Those rats. Probably the ones who conked Radley."

"I found one camera under a door," Chet said. "But the movie equipment's gone." He handed the instrument to Frank.

Frank and Joe decided there was no point in chasing the hoodlums in the darkness. They had too much of a head start. The three boys walked down the rickety stairs to go home. Suddenly an ominous rumble filled the old building. The next moment plaster began falling on their heads. One wall of the stairway was moving inward!

"Run, fellows!" Chet yelled and braced himself

against the wall. "I'll hold this till you're out!"

The Hardys dashed down to the rear entrance. Then Chet took his shoulders from the wall and ran. But he did not have enough time. Wood and plaster filled the stairway.

Frank and Joe turned in horror to see their friend imprisoned in the debris! Only his head showed above the rubble!

The dust and dirt made Chet cough, but he managed to shout, "Help! I'm stuck!"

"Hold on. We'll get you out," Joe cried out.

They clawed at the debris but could make little headway. They needed assistance! While Joe stayed with Chet, Frank raced to the car. On the way to the nearest alarm box, about two blocks down the road, he told Radley what had happened.

"I'll call the police, then drop you off at the hospital," Frank said. "How do you feel now?"

"Not too hot," Radley said weakly.

"By the way, the movie camera's gone. The other one was under a door."

"I hid it there."

"Did you take any photos?"

"Quite a few. Hope they're the ones you want."

Minutes later sirens screamed as Chief Collig and the fire department rushed to the dilapidated building. The men carefully worked their way through the rubble.

Frank returned half an hour later. He and Joe helped under the direction of the fire chief. Huge lights illuminated the area.

"It's touch and go," the official said. "One false move and the whole building could come tumbling down."

Chet's good humor began to abate as the work went on painstakingly slowly.

"I've got an awful pain in my arm," he said. "Maybe it's broken. Frank, better call my parents."

Half an hour later Mr. and Mrs. Morton arrived with Iola, Chet's sister. She was a pretty dark-haired girl who often dated Joe. At the same time, reporters and photographers rushed to the scene where firemen were shoring up the sagging walls with stout beams. Others picked away at the pile of wood, bricks, and plaster.

The Hardys were questioned about the accident. Why were they in the building? Didn't they realize the danger? How did they manage to escape unhurt?

Frank and Joe tried to avoid direct answers, knowing anything they said might tip off their enemies. Joe did, however, tell about Chet's heroic action.

An onlooker, who knew the Hardys, said, "You must be on some detective work. Was it a surveillance?"

"We'd rather not talk about it now," Frank replied. He turned to his brother. "Look, Dad just arrived!"

Mr. Hardy came directly to his sons, who briefed him on the frustrating events. Meanwhile, Chet's spirits had been lifted greatly by the appearance of his family, though he looked pale and wan.

It was long after midnight when the rescuers pulled him from his miserable prison. Two attendants arrived in an ambulance and verified Chet's suspicion about a broken arm. They applied a splint before lifting him into the ambulance, then whisked him off to Bayport Hospital.

His family followed and the Hardys hurried home. In their lab they developed the film expertly, then started to make prints.

"Hey, these are just great!" Frank said as Mr. Hardy looked over his shoulder. Two persons, photographed entering and leaving the premises of Associated Jewelers, were indeed Smith and Jones!

"Now we know for sure they're all in together," the detective said.

After a few hours' sleep and a quick breakfast Mr. Hardy phoned the hospital and learned that Chet was in satisfactory condition and Sam would be released about ten o'clock. Then he and his sons took the photographs to Chief Collig. They were compared with mug shots of known criminals in the area, but to no avail.

"I'll send copies to the FBI in Washington," Collig said. "Maybe they can identify them."

Then the chief drove with the Hardys to Associated Jewelers. The area across the street had been roped off, while workmen razed the remainder of the structure.

The chief tried the door of the office building. It was locked. Frank and Joe went around to look into the windows. "Holy crow!" Frank exclaimed. "They've cleared out. The place is empty!"

The workmen were questioned but had seen nothing.

"Obviously our friends left through the back door," Frank declared.

"Well, Bayport is lucky to be rid of those scoundrels," Chief Collig said.

"But we still have to keep on their trail," Mr. Hardy stated. "I'm sure they'll go to another city, probably even another state, and start all over again with their fraudulent business."

By the time the Hardys returned home, the *Bayport Times* had trumpeted the bravery of Chet Morton all over the front page. Pictures and stories described the disaster and hailed the Hardys' friend as the hero.

"He probably saved our lives," Frank commented.

"And he certainly didn't think about his own safety," Joe added. "Let's hope his arm gets better soon."

The boys notified the Motor Vehicle Bureau of the loss of their driver's licenses and Aunt Gertrude drove them to the agency to get new ones.

Mr. Hardy, meanwhile, called Conrad Greene and spoke to the chess champion's father. When his sons returned, the detective said, "The senior Greene was rather unfriendly and his son won't talk to anyone!"

"Maybe we'd better drive out there and see him personally," Frank said.

Joe nodded. "But first let's visit Chet in the hospital."

The Hardys were surprised to find Krassner sitting at their pal's bedside.

"Hi, Mr. Krassner," Joe greeted him. "What do you think of our hero?"

"He's got plenty of guts," Krassner said admiringly.

"I've also got a cast on my arm that's heavy enough to sink a ship," Chet said. "Here, take a look at this!"

Just then two pretty young nurses entered the room. "Chester, we came to autograph your cast," one of them said.

"Oh sure. Right over here!"

While the girls were inscribing their names,

Chet said, "What about the surveillance, fellows? Get any good shots?"

"I'll say so!" Joe replied. "Great close-ups of Smith and Jones!"

At that moment Frank happened to glance at Krassner. At the mention of Smith and Jones, a fearful expression came over his face!

# CHAPTER IX

## *A Gathering Storm*

FRANK gave his brother a nudge. But Joe had already realized that he should not have talked about their case in front of Krassner.

The man's look of concern now turned into a subdued smile. "I'm glad to see Chet's coming along so well," he said, leaning forward to write his name on the plaster cast. Then he turned to the Hardys. "How about setting a date for visiting me, boys? You wanted to see the Ruby King."

"Sure," Frank said. "Is tomorrow okay with you?"

"That'll be fine. Late in the afternoon."

The young detectives said good-by to their friend, waved to Krassner, then hastened down the hospital corridor. As they were climbing into their car, Frank said, "Krassner must know Smith and Jones. Did you see the look on his face when you mentioned their names?"

Joe nodded. "Sorry I didn't keep my mouth shut."

Frank shrugged. "He seemed to be frightened," he said. "I wonder why."

When they reached home, Fenton Hardy was waiting for them in his study.

"I think we've hit pay dirt," he said. "The FBI has records on Smith and Jones. Smith's real name is Peter Lee Fong. He comes from Hong Kong."

"And Jones?" Joe asked eagerly.

"He's Cyril Eggleby from Kowloon."

"That's near Hong Kong, isn't it?" asked Frank.

"Yes. Right across the harbor. These two are being sought for smuggling operations."

"Smuggling?" Frank looked amazed. "Seems we're on to a big-time racket."

"And a very disturbing one," Mr. Hardy said. "Krassner is a well-known and trusted citizen. How he fits into the picture might prove very embarrassing to him."

"He sure fits in somewhere," Joe said, and mentioned their observation at the hospital.

Mr. Hardy was thoughtful. "Let's review what we know so far. Krassner is afraid of Smith and Jones and has been shot at in the air. Were his attackers Smith and Jones? And why do those two want to bug Conrad Greene's phone? Maybe because he might win the Ruby King. Someone threatens Krassner's life unless he gives up the Ruby King—"

"So it stands to reason," Frank put in excitedly, "that Smith and Jones are Krassner's enemies who are after the chess piece!"

"Wow!" Joe said. "That *is* the logical conclusion. But what do Smith and Jones have to do with Associated Jewelers?"

Mr. Hardy shrugged. "We don't know. And we're not sure if our deductions are correct. Let's think about our next step."

"I'd say we better see Conrad Greene," Frank said.

"What if he won't talk to us?" Joe asked.

"You've got to make him listen somehow," Mr. Hardy said. "Also, I think a surveillance of the area where you saw the serpent balloon is in order."

"Aerial surveillance, Dad?"

"That would be fine. Maybe you can discover its home base. I have to go to New York for a few days. Perhaps I can find out more about Krassner from Wall Street friends while I'm there."

In the interest of speed, it was decided that Frank would go to Ocean Bluffs to see Conrad Greene while Joe would do the surveillance. Frank phoned Biff Hooper, inviting him to come along, and Joe contacted Tony Prito and asked him how he would like to do some flying.

"Sure, when?" Tony asked.

"Tomorrow."

"Something to do with your case?"

"Right. Aerial reconnaisance. I want to look for that serpent balloon."

"What about Frank?"

"He's busy on another angle."

"Okay," Tony said. "When do we meet, and where?"

"At the airport, about ten o'clock."

"I'll be there.'

When Tony showed up at the airport the next morning, he found Joe busy reading weather conditions in the communications office.

"Good flying weather," Joe said. "There's a cold front due later this afternoon, but I don't think it'll bother us."

Outside, Tony squinted up at the clear blue sky. "We're going to have some fun. I'm glad you asked me along."

"Listen, this is no joy ride," Joe reminded him. "We've got a lot of looking to do—but not at the scenery."

When they were airborne, Joe headed first to the area where he and Frank had seen the serpent balloon land at the old farmhouse.

There was no sign of the craft anywhere. "Now what, skipper?" asked Tony from the right-hand seat.

"We'll go to the spot where the shooting took

place. Keep your eyes peeled on the ground."

The two scoured the area, but there was not a trace of the serpent balloon.

Joe crisscrossed back and forth, finally droning over the Morton farm. He flew low and dipped the wings.

"Look, Iola's running out of the house," Tony said.

"I think she knows the sound of our engine," Joe said with a grin as the girl waved up to them. Then he pulled back on the yoke and the plane reached for more altitude.

"Hey, I see something!" Tony cried out suddenly.

Far in the distance a balloon-shaped object seemed to be rising up from the trees. Joe made a beeline for it. Coming closer, both boys started to laugh.

"It's a water tower." Joe chuckled. "Tony, you're a great detective."

They lapsed into serious silence once more. "Can't we get a little rest from all this?" Tony asked finally.

"Okay. I'll take her up high for a while."

The plane gained altitude as Joe flew through a gorgeous cloud which had begun to form in the west. In the brilliant sunshine he guided his craft deftly along the cloud's tumbled slopes, following the ridges, then dropping down to gaps in the fluffy walls.

"Boy, this sure is beautiful," Tony said.

Along the cloud edges, small puffed balls had broken away and Joe felt the wind nudging the plane even higher.

It was then that he noticed a warning sign. In the distance the cloud wall had become black.

"Tony, we'd better get out of here," he said.

"It does look like a storm," Tony agreed, "but it's a long way off."

"Not as far as you might think." Joe glanced down. The ground no longer stood out clearly as before. Long streaks of clouds had slid between the plane and the green woodland. "Oh, oh," he said. "We may be headed for trouble!"

The wind had become rather severe. Joe had to apply extra pressure on the stick and rudder to keep it in level flight. Finally he saw a long cloud canyon ahead of him. It looked like a deep, narrow valley and was what he needed to get down safely. He knew the landmarks well, having flown this area many times before.

Joe glanced at Tony, whose mouth now was set tensely. "Don't panic, we'll make it," he said and pulled on a knob.

Warm air flooded the carburetor system. "That's so we won't ice up," Joe explained. He slid the throttle control back and the roar of the engine became a throaty hum. Then he eased the stick forward and slightly to the left, at the

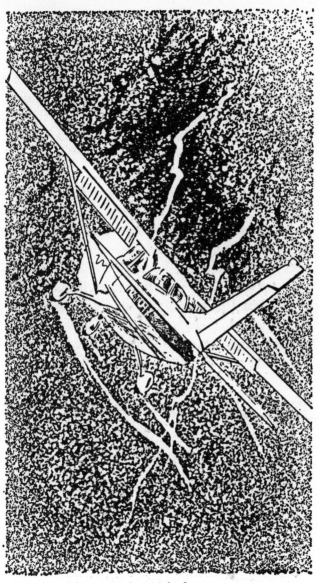

*They were boxed in between two thunderheads!*

same time applying pressure with his left foot to the rudder pedal.

The plane rolled into a wide curving spiral, dropped her nose, and sailed along in a controlled turn toward the earth.

As it rounded the corner of the cloud canyon, Joe suddenly experienced a sick feeling in the pit of his stomach.

*There was no way out!* He was boxed in between two mighty thunderheads—giant cumulonimbus clouds with howling winds and forked spears of lightning!

"Tighten your seat belt, Tony."

The air heaved and rocked the plane. Joe had to hang onto the wheel with all his might to keep it from tearing from his grasp.

Then came a rattle of hail, followed by sheets of rain. It seemed as if they were flying under a waterfall.

"Joe, do you think we'll make it?" Tony asked.

"Start praying, old buddy."

The plane shuddered.

*"Mama mia!"* Tony cried out. "The wings are coming off!"

## CHAPTER X

# *A Strange Hope*

WHILE Joe and Tony struggled for survival in the aerial maelstrom, Frank and Biff drove toward Ocean Bluffs. Halfway there, the same storm which had engulfed the Hardy's plane burst with sudden fury on Biff's car.

First there was a machine-gun rattle of hail, followed by a torrent of rain. The windshield wipers were of little use.

Biff pulled off to the side of the road for a few minutes. "I hope Joe and Tony got back before this storm," he said.

"I wouldn't worry," Frank said. "Joe's a careful pilot."

The thunder and lightning finally subsided and after ten minutes the downpour let up sufficiently for Biff to continue on.

Ocean Bluffs was a small community located on a rocky cove and got its name from cliffs which dropped off quite steeply toward the water. It might have been a popular recreation area if not for the narrow beach. At high tide it was barely more than five feet wide, stony and uneven.

The boys found the home of Conrad Greene close to the ocean, midway between a desolated road and the cliffs. With some difficulty Biff negotiated the muddy driveway and pulled up in front of the house, a low ranch type which sat squat and undistinctive in the driving downpour.

"What an isolated place," Biff said. "It would give me the creeps to live here."

"I guess Conrad likes privacy," Frank said as they made their way over the soggy ground to the front door. There was no bell, so Frank rapped loudly. No answer!

The boy banged again.

"Maybe nobody's home," Biff suggested, turning up his collar to keep the rain from running down his neck.

They were about to leave when the door opened a crack. An elderly man stood behind it.

Frank smiled. "Are you Mr. Greene, Senior?"

"Go away. I don't want to buy anything."

"We're not salesmen. I'm Frank Hardy, and this is my friend Biff Hooper. We'd like to talk to you."

"About what?"

"Look, Mr. Greene, I can't explain while we're drowning. Please let us in!"

"Okay," the man replied grudgingly. "But I'm telling you, I've got nothing to talk about."

By this time Frank and Biff were dripping wet. At the end of a vestibule which led to a large living room, Greene said, "You can dry off, but then you've got to go."

He shuffled into the living room, with the boys following behind him.

"What I want to talk about concerns your son Conrad," said Frank.

"What about him?"

Just then a medium-sized thin man with jet-black hair and a gaunt face appeared from a door on the opposite side of the room.

"Who are these people?" he demanded. "I told you not to let anybody in!"

"They're only going to dry off," the older man said.

"We'd like to talk to you, Mr. Greene," Frank spoke up.

"And we don't want any autograph, either," Biff added, irked by the unfriendly treatment.

"Somebody wants to tap your telephone," Frank began. "Perhaps it's bugged already."

"What?" Conrad Greene now seemed willing to listen.

Frank told about Fenton Hardy's experience with Fong and Eggleby. "Of course my father wouldn't consider doing such a job," he said, "but someone else might not be so ethical."

Color rose to Conrad Greene's pale face. "The Ruby King!" he muttered. "They don't want me to win it!"

"What was that?" Frank asked. "Did you say Ruby King?"

"Forget it," Conrad said curtly. "Can you tell me whether my phone is tapped now?"

Frank, who knew a lot about detection equipment, checked around the house, taking apart the telephone and the single extension. The other three looked on, fascinated by his expertise.

"Seems you're clean," Frank said finally.

By this time the chess master's frigid manner had relaxed somewhat. "I'm glad you came to tell me," he said. "And I hope you'll understand how I feel in regard to strangers—their interminable questions about chess. I lecture, but I don't give individual instruction."

Frank nodded. "By the way, do you ever pass confidential information over the telephone?"

"Yes, as a matter of fact," the man replied. "Being a grandmaster, I often discuss chess with other masters all over the United States."

Frank suggested that perhaps Fong was trying to get some of Greene's strategy on behalf of the opposition. "Or maybe he just wants to snoop into your personal business to psyche you out," he added.

Greene's lips curled in a sly smile. "Nobody

will psyche me. I'm pretty good at that myself."
With that, he said good-by and left the room. His
father escorted the boys to the door.

"I hope my son loses the championship," he
said. "I don't want him to win the Ruby King."

"Why not?" asked Frank.

Mr. Greene did not answer and shut the door
quietly behind the boys. They made their way
to the car. Starting down the driveway, Biff
asked, "Why do you think old Greene doesn't
want his son to win the Ruby King?"

Frank shrugged. "All I can say is that Joe and
I intend to find out about the King pretty soon."
He told Biff about developments in their case
and the husky six-footer was much impressed.

As the boys drove back to Bayport, lacy pat-
terns of lightning were still flickering in the sky
far to the west, indicating that the storm had not
completely passed.

At that very moment Tony Prito was crossing
himself. The Hardys' plane shuddered with teeth-
chattering violence. It lifted like an express elevator, then plunged with a velocity that seemed
to turn Joe's stomach inside out. The wheel was
wrenched from his hands.

"This is the end," he thought.

Suddenly the miracle happened. The plane
dropped down out of the heavy clouds and visi-
bility increased. It was in a spin, heading toward

the hazy green earth below. Joe shook his head to dispel the feeling of dizziness. He grasped the wheel and it responded sluggishly.

Glancing over at Tony, whose eyes were shut tight, Joe said, "You can open them now, pal. We're not going to heaven yet."

But Tony was not ready for quips. Glassy-eyed, he looked straight ahead for several minutes, while Joe brought the craft down even lower, skimming above the dark forest land. Finally Tony said, "That was great handling, Joe."

"Thanks. We were lucky."

Joe nursed the damaged controls, hoping they would stay intact until they reached the airport. It was then that Tony's sharp eyes spied a crude cabin in the woods.

"Hey, look down, Joe! Isn't that a flatbed trailer behind the shack over there?"

"Sure is."

"Can you fly lower for a better look? Maybe it's the hideout of the serpent balloon gang!"

"Sorry, I can't," Joe replied. "The plane's not handling very well. I'll need all the altitude I can get if we have to make an emergency landing."

The shack slid from view and Joe made a beeline for Bayport Airport. He radioed ahead telling the control people he was in trouble.

"Emergency equipment will stand by," came the reply from the tower.

"Hold your hat, Tony," Joe said as they came in for the landing. "I hope this crate sets down in one piece!"

A fire truck and ambulance stood beside the runway, but his skilled handling brought the plane down safely.

Joe and Tony reached the Hardy home minutes before Frank and Biff pulled into the driveway.

Excited conversation ensued for the next hour over sandwiches, then Biff and Tony left and the Hardys arrived at Krassner's place an hour and a half later. They locked the car and walked up to the door.

Krassner met them in the sumptuous foyer, and shook their hands warmly. "Glad you came," he said. "I've taken the Ruby King out of the safe. It's in the library."

Hearing that the valuable antique stood unguarded, Joe frowned.

"I know what you're thinking," Krassner said. "Don't worry. We're alone. I can assure you of that."

He led the way to a wing of the mansion and entered a plush library. Bookstacks extended from the floor to the ceiling, and a dim light filtered through heavy curtains on half-open French doors at the far end of the room.

Suddenly Frank and Joe noticed a shadowy figure standing near the doors!

# CHAPTER XI

## *Over the Cliff*

SUDDEN fear gripped Frank. Had the intruder already raided Krassner's safe? And was he making off with the Ruby King?

Joe's reaction was to dash across the room, but Krassner held him back. "Joe, what are you doing?" he asked. "The King won't run away!"

"Is that the King?" Joe asked in disbelief.

With Frank at his side, he approached the figure cautiously. Now they saw that the chess piece was life-size, intricately carved, and bejeweled with bits of ruby.

"Why—we thought—"

"Yes, that should have occurred to me," Krassner said and chuckled. He parted the curtains, throwing more light on the unusual antique. "You probably assumed the Ruby King was small."

"We did," Frank admitted.

"And made from a solid piece of ruby," Joe added.

The boys walked around the figure, amazed by the subtlety of its carving and the placement of the precious gems. Two of the larger pieces made up the eyes, giving the King a crafty appearance.

"I never knew there were life-size chess pieces," Frank said.

"Oh yes," Krassner told him. "The ancient nobility prized them highly. In several instances the warlords battled over possession of these figures." He went on to explain that the ancients were known even to use people as chess pieces. "Courtyards were laid out as boards," he said, "and the living pieces, usually slaves, moved from one place to another at the master's bidding."

"You know what threw us off," Frank said. "You mentioned keeping the Ruby King in your safe. It must be quite a large one."

Krassner went to the opposite wall, pulled a tapestry aside, and revealed a steel door. The dial was the size of a kitchen plate, and the handle so bulky that it required two strong hands to turn it.

"That's built like a fortress," Joe remarked.

Krassner nodded and pulled the door open. A light sprang on inside and the Hardys looked into the cavernous vault.

"I'd say this is a safe place, wouldn't you?" Krassner said with a self-satisfied smile.

"Where'd you get the design?" Frank quipped. "From Fort Knox?"

Krassner shrugged. "In my business I need a good vault. Now let's put the King in again. Here, Joe, give me a hand."

The boy helped him carry the prize into the safe and Krassner locked the door. Then he put the tapestry back into place and motioned the boys to sit down.

"Well, now you've seen it," he said. "It would be almost impossible to steal, and equally difficult to cart off."

Mr. Hardy had told his sons that no safe ever made was impervious to clever thieves, but Frank and Joe had to admit that Krassner's setup looked pretty tight.

"Matter of fact," the banker went on, "the consortium trusted me with the piece because of my unique vault."

"Mr. Krassner," Frank asked, "how did you acquire the chess piece?"

"It was purchased in China and shipped to this country via Hong Kong."

"Probably smuggled out," Frank thought to himself. He did not quite trust Krassner, and still suspected that the chess piece might have been stolen.

On the way home the boys mused about the Ruby King.

"That was a real shockeroo, wasn't it, Frank?" Joe asked.

"I'll say. Were you going to tackle that wooden dummy?"

"Okay, don't rub it in. I'll bet you thought it was a thief, too."

Frank nodded. "Hey, we're not far from the Morton farm and Chet's home from the hospital. Let's stop in and say hello."

Joe agreed and soon they arrived at the farmhouse. Chet was sitting in the living room watching television.

"Look at this!" Joe quipped. "He's watching kiddie shows!"

Chet was unhappy. "What else can I do? The doctor told me to take it easy for a few days." He sighed. "What's up? Are you breezing around the countryside looking for trouble?"

"Not exactly," Frank said. "We were looking at a life-size chess king."

Iola had come in and overheard the last sentence. "What?" she said in surprise. "Is there really such a thing?"

"Yes. And it came all the way from China."

"Tell me more."

"Unfortunately that's all we know."

Iola looked thoughtful. "I might be able to find out more about ancient chess pieces. Would that be of any help to you?"

"Sure. How are you going to do it?"

"Oh, leave it to me," Iola said coyly.

On the way home, Frank said, "I wonder what Iola has in mind."

"She's pretty smart," Joe said. "Don't worry about it."

As they pulled into the driveway, Frank said, "Joe, I've been thinking."

"About what?"

"Conrad Greene's place. Maybe the wiretap is on the outside of the house!"

"You only checked indoors?"

"Yes. It didn't occur to me until just now."

"Then let's take a look tomorrow morning."

"Okay. We'll phone him tonight."

After dinner Frank called the Greene residence. Conrad's father answered, saying it was all right to come the next day and check the outside.

"This time you won't get wet, either." He chuckled. "The weather bureau predicted sunshine."

When Frank asked about Conrad, he learned that the champion was out of town conducting an exhibition tour.

"He plays ten games simultaneously—and blindfolded!" Mr. Greene said proudly.

Frank thanked him and hung up. When he told Joe about the grandmaster's exhibition, the boy whistled. "Wow! I've trouble playing one opponent with my eyes open!"

"You're not a genius, Joe. I keep telling you that."

Joe gave his brother a good-natured poke in the ribs. "Well, let's see what kind of a genius you are in solving our new mystery."

The boys waited until ten-thirty the next morning, thinking their father might call from New York, but finally Frank said, "We'd better be on our way. I wanted to tell Dad about the Ruby King, but it'll have to wait."

The day was bright and clear. On the highway a black sedan kept behind them for a while, and Joe became suspicious. A man and a woman were in the car. But it turned off onto a side road before they reached Ocean Bluffs.

The elder Mr. Greene let them in and Frank introduced his brother.

"How's that big fellow who was with you. What's his name? Boff?"

"Oh, you mean Biff. He's fine. Mr. Greene, may we check in the house again for any bugs? Then we'll investigate outside. It could be they have tapped your line by the pole near the road."

"Sure. Go ahead."

The boys went to work with speedy efficiency. "Nothing here," Joe said finally. As they moved toward the front door, a shrill scream pierced the stillness.

The boys ran outside, followed by the old man. They saw a woman running frantically toward the steeply sloping cliff. A man was chasing her!

Suddenly she whirled about and in a high-pitched voice shouted, "I'll throw myself into the sea if you come one step further!"

The man hesitated, then started his pursuit again.

"Do you think it's a lovers' quarrel?" Joe asked.

"Whatever it is, it could have serious consequences. That woman might kill herself!"

The Hardys raced up to the man. "Hold it!" Frank called out. "Leave her alone!"

"You take care of him," Joe said to his brother. "I'll try to keep the woman from jumping off." He rushed toward the cliff.

"What's going on?" Frank asked the man.

"Don't let her do it!" he panted, throwing up his arms in despair. "She's crazy enough to do anything!"

Joe, meanwhile, had reached the woman, who stood precariously close to the edge of the cliff. He put both arms around her waist and began pulling her back. Suddenly she spun around. Now Joe was at the lip of the cliff himself! The woman tried to shove him over, and in her efforts a wig fell off her head!

"Holy crow!" Joe thought. "It's a man!"

Frank was having his troubles, too. The man, who had pleaded for help a moment before, set upon him and wrestled him toward the cliff. In the distance, Mr. Greene wrung his hands in despair. "They're trying to shove you over!" he cried out.

This was painfully evident to the Hardy boys, who had a tough fight on their hands. Frank got the better of his adversary with a karate chop. The man staggered, then ran back toward the driveway.

Frank rushed forward to help his brother. Both Joe and his adversary were still wrestling at the lip of the cliff. Suddenly, to Frank's horror, both fell over and rolled down the steep embankment, locked together in a bear hug!

As they tumbled down the sandy, rocky slope, Frank saw that the other man was getting the worst of it. His head crashed against one rock, then another. By the time both hit the narrow beach a hundred feet below, they rolled apart and lay motionless.

Frank's adversary had reached his car which was parked down the road and drove off. It was a black sedan! "We were followed after all," Frank thought to himself.

He turned to Mr. Greene, who had come up alongside him. "They're hurt," the boy said. "Is there a way to the beach?"

The elderly man pointed to a narrow, rutted lane some distance away, which twisted steeply

to the water's edge. "It hasn't been used in years,"
he said. "Part of it's been washed away by rain."

"I'm going down," Frank said. "Better call an
ambulance."

When Frank reached the bottom he raced over
to his brother. Joe was just opening his eyes.

"You all right?" Frank asked, his throat dry.

Joe stood up cautiously and moved his arms
and legs. "I guess so. Don't think I broke anything. But this other character might not be so
well off."

The boys walked over to Joe's adversary. He
was lying on his side.

"Better not touch him," Frank warned. "He
might be in serious trouble."

They bent down to get a look at the man's
face.

"Good grief!" Frank said. "It's Gerard Henry!"

"The jewelry salesman?"

"That's right."

Frank and Joe splashed water on Henry's face,
but the man did not revive.

Just then two policemen carrying a stretcher
came down the narrow trail.

"I'm Lieutenant Skillman," one of them introduced himself. "And this is Officer Gray. What
happened?"

Frank told him quickly. "He's still unconscious," the young detective concluded.

The officers carefully moved the man and put him on the stretcher. Then they carried him up the cliff, while Frank helped Joe, who was still shaky and hurting.

A police ambulance stood at the Greenes' house, and Gerard Henry was lifted into it. Joe noticed that one of his ladies' shoes was missing.

"The wig got lost, too," he commented wryly.

Just then the "phony lady" came to. He rolled his eyes and sat up, looking ludicrous in his dress. He shook his head to clear the cobwebs.

Lieutenant Skillman advised the man of his rights and began questioning him, but Henry's jaw was set tight and he refused to say anything. Frank and Joe, who had already told what had happened, filled the officers in on Henry's part in the jewelry racket.

"Will you press charges for assault and battery?" Skillman asked the boys.

"With intent to kill!" Frank declared.

"All right. You'll be called as witnesses." Skillman handcuffed Gerard Henry and made him lie down in the ambulance.

"We only have a small jail in Ocean Bluffs," he said, "but I think it'll be adequate. As soon as you're released from the hospital, that's where you'll go."

Mr. Greene shook his head in disbelief as they walked back toward the house. "You boys sure got into a lot of trouble on our account," he said. "Why do you suppose those men were trying to throw you over the cliff?"

"To get us out of the way for some reason," Joe said.

"Let's take a look at that telephone pole," Frank said. When they reached the end of the drive he climbed partly up the base of the pole. It was covered with creosote and tar.

"What a mess," he grumbled as he climbed higher. At the junction he examined the wires and called down: "Here's the tap, Joe. What'll we do with it?"

"Listen, Frank, I've got an idea," Joe called up. "Why don't we leave it and tell Conrad to pass on false information as to how he would tackle different problems in chess? He can get in touch with his partners on a public telephone and clue them in."

"Not bad," Frank agreed. "It would confuse his enemies."

When he came down, Mr. Greene chuckled. "Hey, this is like reading a detective story," he said. "I'm sure Conrad will go along with your strategy."

It was early afternoon when the Hardys arrived home. They were met at the kitchen door by Aunt Gertrude. A look of horror crossed her face when she saw them.

"Oh, Frank, Joe!" she shrieked.

## CHAPTER XII

## *The King's Curse*

FRANK felt the blood drain from his face. "What's happened? Is Dad all right?"

"Nothing's happened to your father," Aunt Gertrude said tartly. "But look at you—you're a mess! Filthy, and your face is scratched, and Joe's clothes are torn and he's bruised all over—"

"Is that all?" Frank interrupted, heaving a sigh of relief. "We thought the sky had fallen in."

Hearing the commotion, Mrs. Hardy entered the kitchen. Worriedly she scrutinized the boys, then said, "You do look pretty bad. Are you sure you're not hurt?"

"Frank's dirty because he climbed a telephone pole," Joe said, "and I'm a little sore from fighting a lady that was no lady. But everything's okay, Mother."

"Have crooks been chasing you?" Aunt Gertrude demanded. Without waiting for an answer, she said. "Of course they have. Where were you?"

Frank told their story and finally managed to calm his excited aunt. "Did you hear from Dad?" he asked.

"Yes, we did," Mrs. Hardy replied.

"Has he had any luck?"

"He said he was making good headway, that's all."

The boys went up to their room and soon returned with clean clothes. They handed the dirty ones to their mother.

"Let me put some antiseptic on your scratches," Mrs. Hardy said.

She went to the bathroom to deposit the clothes in the hamper and returned with the liquid. While she pressed soaked cotton swabs against the boys' injuries, Frank dialed police headquarters.

"Hi, Chief. Frank Hardy. I've got some good news. The Ocean Bluffs police captured Gerard Henry."

"He's a slick operator," the chief replied. "How'd they do it?"

Frank told of their adventure and how they had left the wiretap in place in order to mislead Conrad Greene's enemies.

Collig thanked him for his information. "I'll get in touch with Lieutenant Skillman," he said. "We can tack a few more charges onto that hoodlum."

"Like fraud, you mean?"

"That's right. Let me know if anything further develops, Frank."

The hungry boys had just finished a snack when a youth about eighteen came to the door. He had an envelope marked Bayport Museum for the Hardys.

Frank took it and the messenger hurried off.

"Hey, Joe. I wonder what this is all about," Frank said and slit open the envelope. On a piece of museum stationery was typed:

> Frank and Joe Hardy:
> May have some information to help you.
>                                    Ruby King

"Is this some kind of a gag?" Joe asked.

"It may be a trap," Frank said. "We're pretty good at falling into those lately, you know."

"Not this time," Joe said. "Let's call the museum and ask about this Ruby King."

Frank did not like the idea. "It might be like phoning the zoo and asking for Mr. Fox," he said. "We'll go over ourselves tomorrow morning."

"But not without bodyguards!"

The Hardys decided to phone their backup team of Biff Hooper, Tony Prito, and Phil Cohen. The latter was a slight, intense boy with a razor-sharp mind.

The three friends readily agreed to meet the boys next morning and serve as lookouts around the museum.

When they rendezvoused at nine o'clock, Joe looked at the austere stone building without windows and said, "Not a very inviting place. When I was a little kid, I used to think this was a mausoleum."

Biff, Tony, and Phil stationed themselves on the outside. They would go in if the Hardys were not back in fifteen minutes.

Frank and Joe bounded up the marble steps and opened the heavy bronze door. Inside sat a blond young woman behind the information desk.

"We're here to see Ruby King," Frank said.

"You'll find Mrs. King down the hall in the room marked *Ancient Art*."

"You mean there really is a Ruby King?" Joe asked.

The receptionist cocked her head and looked at the Hardys quizzically. "What made you think there wasn't?"

"Oh, nothing," Joe muttered. The boys found the proper door and entered a large high-ceilinged room. In it were plaster facades of ancient buildings, glass cases filled with artifacts, tapestries, and a few paintings.

Their eyes swept the room, finally coming to rest on a small desk in one corner. Behind it sat a buxom, dark-haired woman. She wore a blue dress and eyeglasses. Her hair was piled high on her head. She smiled as the boys approached.

"You must be Frank and Joe Hardy."

"Yes," Joe said, surprised, as the woman continued, "You're detectives, interested in an ancient Chinese chess piece."

Frank laughed. "I think you're the detective, Mrs. King. By the way, is that really your name?"

"Of course it is. I was born Ruby Smith, but when I married Mr. King, I got the name of the famous chess piece."

Mrs. King explained that she had been hired recently from the Museum of Natural History in New York City to become a curator in Bayport. "Oriental art is my field, and I understand you'd like to know more about this particular antique."

Suddenly an idea occurred to Frank. "Did Iola Morton tell you?"

"That's right. She was in yesterday."

"You're very kind to take such an interest," Joe said.

The curator said that the piece had been made in India and carried by caravan to China during the Ming Dynasty. "Of course, it was part of a complete set," she explained.

"So we heard," Frank said.

"But did you hear about the curse?"

"A curse, really?" asked Joe.

"Every person who has come into possession of the Ruby King has died under unusual and tragic circumstances," Mrs. King went on. "The first warlord who owned the piece was struck by lightning the day after he acquired it. Another owner died from poison a week after he bought the King, a third drowned in a flood which carried the Ruby King all the way down the Yangtze River."

"Then what happened to it?" asked Frank.

"It was found by a poor peasant who was gored to death by a bull the next day."

"Then Mr. Krassner better look out," Joe said. "Do you really believe these fairy tales, Mrs. King?"

"Maybe they're only legends," the woman replied. "But I thought you'd like to know about them." She went on to tell the boys about the game of chess, which originated in India. *"Shah mat* means *The king is dead,"* she said. "That's where we get the word checkmate. The German word for it is *Schach matt."*

While the boys listened intently, Tony, Biff, and Phil waited impatiently outside.

"Wonder what's taking them so long," said Biff.

"Maybe they got conked," Tony said.

"Let's go in and take a look," Phil suggested. "The fifteen minutes are almost up."

The three went inside and were greeted with the same hospitality as the Hardys. When they asked about their friends, they were directed to the room of Ancient Art.

"Let's enter one at a time," Biff said. "Phil, you go first. If there's any trouble, whistle."

Phil went in. As he approached the group, Mrs.

King was saying, "The curse can be lifted, according to an old story."

"How?" asked Frank, waving to Phil.

"If it's buried."

Joe let out a low whistle. Biff and Tony burst into the room, glancing wildly about. But Phil motioned with his hands. "Calm down, fellows, everything's all right."

"What's going on?" Mrs. King asked, surprised.

The three boys were introduced and the whole thing explained. She laughed, and they resumed their conversation.

"If the curse can be lifted, why didn't one of the previous owners bury the King?" Joe asked.

"That's the point," the curator went on. "It must not be buried by the owner, or anyone who knows him."

"How is that possible?" Frank asked.

Mrs. King shrugged. "That's all I can tell you about the Ruby King. Has it been of any help?"

"Very much so," Frank said.

They thanked the woman and left, their footsteps echoing along the marble corridor.

Outside, the Hardys discussed what they had just heard, then Frank said, "Are you fellows busy this afternoon? I'd like to check out that cabin in the woods. Want to help?"

The answer was an enthusiastic Yes.

"Good idea," Joe said. "But first, how about some chow at our house?"

After lunch of roast-beef sandwiches, topped off with wedges of Aunt Gertrude's apple pie, the boys drove off to look for the shack which Joe and Tony had discovered in their horrendous aerial search.

It took more than an hour before they found the small country road which led to the old cabin. Biff parked and they proceeded on foot, peering out from the trees to observe the solitary building.

"It looks deserted," Joe whispered.

The windows were boarded up. Weeds grew high around the walls, and the cabin gave the appearance of having been abandoned long ago.

As the boys were about to go closer, Phil whispered, "Duck!"

Everyone dropped to the ground, and five pairs of prying eyes watched a man sneak out of the woods.

"He looks like Eggleby," Joe whispered.

The man knocked on the door and said, *"Shah mat!"*

A bolt clicked and he was let in.

The boys conversed in low tones about what to do next.

"If that was really Eggleby, he might know us," Frank said. "Tony, you and Phil go up and knock at the door. Give the password. We'll back you up in case of trouble."

"Okay. Here goes," Tony said. He and Phil crept from their hiding place, walked across a small open area, and knocked on the door. *"Shah mat!"* Phil said.

The door opened and they were admitted into the dark interior. All became quiet—ominously quiet, Frank thought. After ten minutes, neither of the two boys had returned.

"Something fishy's going on in there," Joe said. "I think we'd better take a look-see."

"All right," Frank agreed. "Come on."

The Hardys and Biff went to the door, knocked, and Frank said in a loud voice, *"Shah mat!"*

There was no answer. Joe tried the doorknob. It was locked.

"Stand back," Biff said. He leaped forward and banged his shoulder against the door. It gave way with a cracking sound, and the boys dashed inside. It took a few seconds for their eyes to become adjusted to the dark interior.

"Good night!" Frank said. "They're all gone!"

# CHAPTER XIII

## *The Third Man*

"THEY'VE vanished!" Biff exclaimed. "Disappeared into thin air!"

"There must be another way out," Frank declared, moving around.

"All the windows are barred and there's no back door," Joe observed.

"Maybe there's a trap door," Biff suggested.

The three got on their hands and knees, probing along the wooden floor with their fingers.

"Here's something," Frank said as he felt a small, countersunk hinge.

In the shaft of light coming through the door, the boys made out the thin outline of a small trap door, barely large enough to admit a broad-shouldered person. Biff pried it open with his pocketknife and lowered himself into the hole, which was about five feet deep.

He groped about, finally locating an opening into the hard-packed earth. "Hey, guys, it's a tunnel!" Biff said.

"Can you get through?" Frank asked.

"Just about."

"Okay, go ahead. I'll follow you. Joe, better stay topside, just in case."

"Okay," Joe said.

Frank dropped down into the hole, found the opening, and proceeded to wriggle through behind Biff. Bits of dirt fell on top of the boys as they inched forward. The air grew heavy, redolent of musty soil.

Biff stopped momentarily. "Are you coming, Frank?" His muffled words sounded like a voice from a tomb.

"Yes. Go ahead. But don't press against the roof too hard."

While the two continued to mole their way through the dank tunnel, Joe stepped outside the cabin and listened. Except for birds twittering, no sound came from the surrounding woods.

"I wonder where they'll finally exit," the boy mused.

Ten minutes later Biff called back to Frank again, "I see the light up ahead."

"Okay, Biff. I'm right behind you."

Now the tunnel widened considerably and the boys scrambled side by side toward the end. Just before they reached it, they came upon Phil and

Tony. They were tied hand and foot and gagged, and trussed up in such a way that the least movement would choke them.

Frank and Biff tore off their gags and cut the ropes. "You okay?" Frank asked anxiously.

Tony nodded, sat up, and said weakly, "They're getting away. Outside—look!"

Frank and Biff rushed from the exit, which proved to be the mouth of a cave, and found themselves in a wide clearing. Suddenly they heard the engine of a car. Through the leafy branches of low-hanging trees they could make out a black sedan as it started along a rutted trail. Three men were in it!

Phil and Tony had followed the boys and staggered toward them.

"Were those the three guys who conked you?" Frank asked, pointing to the car.

"Only two did," Phil said.

"Then the third man must have been a lookout at the end of the tunnel," Frank conjectured.

"Where's Joe?" Tony asked.

"Back at the cabin. I'll have to give him the signal." Frank imitated the cry of a bird.

Joe heard it faintly and repeated it. He started out across the woods, reaching the clearing a few minutes later.

"Those two had weapons," Phil said. "They made us crawl through the tunnel, and when we neared the end, they gagged us and tied us up."

The boys walked back through the woods to make a thorough search of the cabin.

"I guess they cleaned it out completely," Frank said. "Joe, did you look around outside?"

"Yes, but I didn't have time to check in the back."

"Okay, let's do it now," Frank said, and led the others through the door and to the rear of the cabin.

Phil noticed something far off in the weeds. "What's that?" he asked, running toward it. He reached into the tall grass and pulled at a dirty tarpaulin. Beneath it was a neatly packed balloon!

Within minutes, the boys had spread open the envelope. "It's the serpent!" Joe exclaimed.

"What a find!" Tony said.

"We'll take it to the police as evidence," Frank decided. "It's the balloon from which we were shot at!"

As they repacked the nylon envelope, Tony spied a piece of paper which apparently had fallen from the folds.

"Frank, Joe, look at this!"

"What is it?" Frank asked.

"A cablegram from Hong Kong!"

The boys crowded around as Tony read the message aloud: " 'Ming Do very ill. Hurry via Queen. Serpents.' "

"What do you suppose that means?" Phil asked.

The Hardys studied the cable carefully and

Frank said, "A person named Ming Do wants someone to hurry by the way of Queen something or other."

"And Serpents means the serpent gang," Biff added.

"But what is Queen? Is that some kind of code word?" Joe wondered.

"The balloon won't fit in the car," Tony said. "I'll drive back to town and get our pickup."

"Good idea," Frank said and handed him the keys.

Tony returned shortly and the boys loaded up the balloon. On the way back to Bayport, they speculated about the turn of events. The evidence they had found certainly advanced the Hardys' case. Or perhaps, as Frank secretly thought, it had plunged them even deeper into an insoluble mystery!

When they arrived at police headquarters, Chief Collig was amazed to hear their story. He accepted the serpent balloon as evidence and looked at the cable.

"Whoever they're talking about is going to Hong Kong soon," he conjectured. "If only we had a way to stop him. But we don't even know who's involved!"

He shook his head slowly. "I have some news, too," he continued. "Not good, I'm afraid."

"What happened?" Joe asked.

*"Frank, Joe, look at this!"* Tony said.

"Gerard Henry escaped from the Ocean Bluffs jail."

"How'd he do that?" Biff asked.

Collig said that Henry had feigned illness and fooled an inexperienced guard. When his cell was opened, he had jumped the officer, disarmed him, and raced right out the front door.

"Listen," Joe said. "Do you suppose he was that third man in the woods?"

"Might have been," Collig said.

After they had made their report, the Hardys thanked their friends for their help. "We couldn't have pulled this off without you," Frank said.

"You'll make detectives out of us yet," Tony said as he drove them back to his house where he had left the Hardys' car.

Frank and Joe decided to visit Krassner in his office to tell him that his tormentors had apparently fled. And perhaps the man could shed some light on the mysterious cable. On the way they dropped Phil off at his house.

Krassner occupied a suite in Bayport's newest office building and received the boys cordially.

"We've got some exciting news for you," Joe said.

The financier looked pleased, but as the story unfolded, his face clouded with fear and apprehension. When Frank mentioned the contents of the cable, Krassner paled.

"Call my wife!" he ordered his secretary. When

she reported that his home phone was dead, Krassner jumped up. "The worst has happened!" he cried and ran outside.

Frank and Joe followed him, trying to find out what had upset him so.

"Later," Krassner said. He leaped behind the wheel of his sports car and started the engine. Then he drove off.

Frank and Joe took their own car and followed. "Do you think he's going home?" Joe asked.

"Looks that way," Frank replied. "Funny. We never saw his wife. I didn't think he had one."

"Maybe he feels she's in danger," Joe said.

They pulled into Krassner's driveway directly behind him and the three hurried into the house. The banker called for his wife, but she was not there.

"It's the servants' day off, too," Krassner said, rushing into the library. He tried the handle to his vault. It was locked.

"Maybe the worst hasn't happened after all," Joe said. "That is, if you were talking about the theft of the Ruby King."

Krassner did not reply. With trembling fingers he dialed the combination, turned the handle, and pulled open the steel door. Everyone gasped.

*The Ruby King was gone!*

## CHAPTER XIV

## *The Oriental Connection*

FOOTSTEPS sounded and a woman entered the library. She was slightly built, with a calm and lovely Oriental face.

"Albert! What happened?" She looked at Krassner in alarm. He stood as if in a trance in front of the yawning vault.

His mouth moved, but no words came out.

"The King has disappeared," Joe explained. "Are you Mrs. Krassner?"

"Yes. Oh dear!" The woman stepped forward and put an arm around her husband, who finally regained enough composure to talk.

"What'll I do?" he repeated over and over. "What'll I do?"

Frank turned to the woman, who tried to calm her husband. "Did you just come home, Mrs. Krassner?"

"Yes. I left this morning to visit a friend."

"Did you see anything unusual when you left?"

The woman thought for a moment, then she said, "Yes, two men. They were in a car near the entrance to our driveway."

"Did you get a good look at them?" Joe asked.

"Their faces were turned away."

"Weren't you suspicious?"

"No. Not really. People often stop to admire our place."

Frank took his brother aside and spoke to him quietly. "Those two men probably were Fong and Eggleby. And the Ruby King might be what Ming Do wants!"

"It wouldn't surprise me!"

Mrs. Krassner summoned the Franklin Township Police, and they arrived in a few minutes to look for clues. Fingerprints were found on the safe, but they proved to be those of Krassner, who by now had gone to his bedroom in a virtual state of collapse.

After calling a doctor, Mrs. Krassner thanked the boys and ushered them to the door. Outside, they were startled to see their father drive up.

"Dad! When did you get back?" Frank asked.

"About an hour and a half ago. Mother said you had gone to see Mr. Krassner. I called his office and was told all three of you had dashed out of there in a hurry because his home phone was dead. It sounded like trouble so I came out." Mr. Hardy pointed to the police car. "I take it the Ruby King has been stolen."

Joe nodded. "Dad, we've got an awful lot to tell you."

"I have some news, too," Mr. Hardy said. "Let's stop at the next diner and talk."

Frank and Joe led the way in their car until they came to a new restaurant at a traffic circle. They pulled into the parking lot and their father followed.

Inside, they found a comfortable isolated booth, where nobody could overhear their conversation. Frank and Joe ordered hamburgers and coke, while Mr. Hardy was content with a cup of coffee.

"Wait till you hear about Mrs. Krassner!" Joe said after a waitress had taken their order. "She's—"

"Chinese," Mr. Hardy said.

"How'd you know?"

"I found out in New York. Also learned a few other tidbits."

"Come on, Dad, out with it!" Joe urged.

"For one thing, Krassner is originally from Hong Kong. One of his grandmothers was a Chinese, which makes him one fourth Oriental."

"So that's what gives him that odd look," Frank said.

"His wife's family," Mr. Hardy went on, "is very prominent in Hong Kong circles. Her father is Moy Chen-Chin, a social big wheel and very rich."

"So now the chop suey thickens," Joe quipped. "What else?"

As the boys munched their hamburgers, Mr. Hardy filled them in on Krassner's career. "As a youth, he got involved in a smuggling ring. His father-in-law got him out of that scrape and Krassner came to this country. He's been a citizen of the United States for the past twenty years."

"Funny," Frank said. "I never quite trusted him."

"He's been straight ever since and has a fine record as an investment banker. Much of his work involves Oriental securities," Mr. Hardy said.

"And his father-in-law is his Oriental connection," Joe put in. "No doubt an invaluable asset."

"Wait a minute," Frank said. "There was no sign of forced entry in this theft. Maybe Krassner returned to his crooked ways and stole the piece himself! Was it insured?"

"You caught on fast. Yes. He took out a large policy on the Ruby King several weeks ago," Mr. Hardy said.

Joe looked dubious. "I can't quite believe that. I have another theory."

"What's that?" Frank asked.

"Krassner was intimidated by Fong and Eggleby. We know that he was afraid of them. Maybe they discovered his past and threatened to expose him unless he handed over the Ruby King!"

"Could be," Frank said. "That would be a better reason for his not wanting to go to the police. I never believed his story that he was afraid of the publicity. After all, he was the official custodian of this valuable antique. Just because someone was after it, Krassner's reputation wouldn't have been ruined!"

Mr. Hardy nodded. "Of course anyone buying an expensive object like that would insure it properly. I tend to agree with Joe's reasoning."

"Our next step is to find the King," Frank said. "And we'd better be fast about it or Ming Do will get it."

Mr. Hardy looked puzzled, and the boys clued him in on their adventure in the woods, the cable they had found, and Mrs. King's information on the old chess piece.

Mr. Hardy was thoughtful for a while, then he said, "The most logical way of transporting an item like that would be by sea. Perhaps there's a ship in the harbor named *Queen!*"

"Let's go home and call the harbor master," Frank urged, and stood up.

Mr. Hardy paid the bill and soon they were on their way. It was dark when they turned into Elm Street and they were surprised to see their security spotlights casting a dazzling glow all around the house.

"Oh, oh, something's happened," Joe said as Frank drove toward the garage. An alarm bell was ringing.

"Something's definitely wrong," Frank said.

All three jumped out of their cars and raced inside. Joe shut off the electronic alarm system, then followed his father and Frank into the living room, where Mrs. Hardy and Aunt Gertrude rose to meet them.

"Laura, what's the matter?" Mr. Hardy asked.

"We're a little frightened, Fenton."

"I'm scared to death!" Aunt Gertrude said. "It's on account of those terrible criminals."

"Easy," Frank said. "Just tell us from the beginning."

"We received a package!" Aunt Gertrude pointed to a cardboard shoe box lying on the coffee table. Frank went to open it.

"Don't touch it! You'll get bitten!"

"By what?"

"A snake! A big venomous snake!" Gertrude Hardy cried.

Mrs. Hardy spoke up. "It's not really big, and I don't think it's poisonous. But you never can tell."

"How'd you get it?" Joe asked.

Mrs. Hardy said it was delivered to the door shortly after dark. "We jumped out of our skin when we opened it," she concluded.

Frank set the box on the floor and took the lid

off. Inside lay a small garter snake. He picked it up and it crawled over his hand and up his left arm. "I'll take it out in the yard," he said.

"No doubt it was a warning from the serpent gang," Mr. Hardy said.

"Fenton, you'd better drop this case while we're still healthy!" his sister implored him.

"If I dropped my cases because of threats, I'd soon be out of business," Mr. Hardy said. "But let's turn the alarm system on again, just to be on the safe side."

"Now that the Serpents have the Ruby King, why are they still bothering us?" Frank asked.

"They know we'll keep after them and might nail them yet," Joe said.

Mr. Hardy put in a call to the harbor master's office. "They'll check and let us know," he told his sons after he had finished.

The next morning during breakfast the phone rang. Frank took it, listened tensely for a few seconds, then hung up.

"Guess what!" he said. "There's a Japanese ship in the harbor that's due to sail day after tomorrow at midnight."

"Where to?" Joe asked.

"Hong Kong. And her name's *Queen Maru!*"

# CHAPTER XV

## *Faked Out!*

"THAT's the *Queen* mentioned in the cablegram!" Joe exclaimed. "It has to be!"

Frank was skeptical. "I doubt that the Serpents would be that obvious about it."

"I'm convinced," Joe said. "I'll bet that Fong and Eggleby are still in the area and they plan to ship the Ruby King on the *Queen Maru*."

"It's a strong possibility," Mr. Hardy agreed. "Better drive down to the harbor and take a look at the *Queen Maru*."

Before the boys left, the phone rang again. It was Conrad Greene's father. He told Joe that his son was still on the chess exhibition tour. "He's due to play in Bayport tomorrow night," Mr. Greene said, "at the VFW Hall."

"Thanks for letting us know," Joe said. "We'd like to see the match."

Half an hour later, Frank and Joe arrived at the

dock and parked near the *Queen Maru*. On her deck giant booms were hoisting heavy machinery into her hold.

The Hardys climbed the gangway, asked for the captain, and were directed to a neat forward cabin. At the door they were greeted by a short, smiling, barrel-chested Japanese named Taro Ono.

"May I help you?" he asked cordially.

The boys explained they were detectives and were looking for a wooden box, roughly two-feet-two by six, containing contraband destined for Hong Kong.

"About the size of a coffin," Captain Ono said, stroking his chin. "No. We carry only large crates of machinery, as you can see for yourself."

"Are you sure?"

"I know my cargo well," the captain answered, still maintaining his pleasant look.

"Well, thank you, sir," Frank said and the boys clambered down the steel gangway to the dock.

"Now what?" Joe asked.

"The ship doesn't leave till tomorrow night. We'll have to keep a constant watch on it."

Joe sighed. "Okay. Let's get our reinforcement team for help."

Biff, Phil, Tony, and the Hardys staked out the freighter all day and night. No suspicious box was loaded and nothing unusual happened. Tony had drawn the late-night shift, and Frank and Joe arrived in the morning to spell him. After a few encouraging words from their tired pal, they settled in a strategic spot and prepared for a long wait.

About ten o'clock an old hearse drove up next to the freighter. At the wheel was a youth not much older than the Hardys. He hopped out, opened the back of the hearse, and began pulling out a pine box.

"Joe! We might have hit pay dirt!" Frank said excitedly.

"Come on, Frank. Let's find out and ask this character a few questions!"

Frank and Joe ran up to the youth. "You work for an undertaker?" Frank asked.

"No. What's it to you, anyhow?"

"Where'd you get the hack?" Joe asked.

"At the junkyard. Not bad, eh? The girls really like it. Say, who are you guys?"

Frank told him. "And what's your name?"

"Oscar."

"If you don't work for an undertaker, Oscar," Joe said, "what are you doing delivering a coffin?"

"Oh, is this a coffin?" The youth eased it onto the dock.

"Don't try to be funny," Frank said. "We want straight answers."

"Okay, okay. So I'm delivering a coffin," Oscar said. "Some Oriental-looking guy asked me to bring it to this ship. And he paid me twenty-five bucks. That's all I know. Why don't you get off my back?"

"You can't deliver a corpse without a license," Joe said.

"I'm getting out of here!" Oscar slid in beside the wheel and started off as Frank jotted down his license number.

Joe sat on the pine box while Frank went to call Chief Collig. When the policeman arrived with another officer, Joe related their suspicion that the Ruby King was hidden in the wooden box.

"We can find out soon enough," Collig said. He ordered the policeman to open the box, the lid of which was fastened by eight screws.

The officer got a screwdriver from the trunk of the squad car and went to work.

Finally he was finished. The Hardys held their breath as the top was removed. Then they let out a groan!

*Inside lay a five-foot log!*

Chief Collig turned the piece of wood over and examined it. "This doesn't look like contraband, fellows," he said.

Meanwhile, Captain Ono had noticed the police and came off his ship to investigate. When asked about the box, he denied any knowledge of the strange cargo.

"What am I supposed to do?" he asked, puzzled. "I can't load it without papers."

"Don't worry about it," Chief Collig said. "You're not loading it at all. I'm taking it to headquarters." He turned to the boys. "We'll give it the once-over in the lab. I'll let you know if we find any clues."

"Thanks, Chief," Frank said.

Then Frank and Joe discussed the ruse. "When the gang suspected that we had found the cable," Joe said, "they must have figured we'd be watching the ship. So they went to all this trouble to keep us here, meanwhile transporting the Ruby King some other way."

"Such as?"

"Such as by airplane!"

"We should have thought of that before!" Frank said. "Come on. Let's call the airport!"

At home the boys took turns telephoning all the airlines using the local terminal. One after another the replies were negative. No coffins had been shipped out. No rectangular boxes, nothing to indicate that the Ruby King had been flown away.

"Here's a strictly freight service," Frank said, scanning the phone book. "Premier Airways." He called the number and talked with a friendly agent. Two coffins had been transported to the West Coast the day before. Both were from local morticians and had been properly documented.

Frank pressed further. "We're looking for a wooden figure. Very valuable. That's why it was stolen."

"Oh, stolen goods! We'd like to help you, but— Hold on. Could it have been hidden in a rug?"

"Sure could! Was a rug part of your cargo?"

"Yes, yesterday. A large one, wrapped in heavy brown paper. One end was torn, and now that you mention it, I saw something wooden showing through."

"Where was the destination?" Frank's heart thumped with excitement.

"Wait a minute, I'll check." The answer came shortly. "We shipped the rug non-stop to San Francisco. Final destination was Hong Kong!"

"Then it's out of the country by now," Frank said.

"Sure. Matter of fact, it must have arrived about a half hour ago."

Frank thanked the clerk and hung up, shaking his head. "Boy, did we get faked out! Now what are we going to do?"

"Call Chief Collig," Joe suggested and dialed headquarters. After he told the chief the bad news, Collig said, "This isn't our day. I just learned that Gerard Henry was seen in town the night before last. But he slipped away before we could apprehend him."

Frank and Joe sat in gloomy silence until Joe suggested they have some lunch. As they were eating their sandwiches, Chet walked in the back door.

"Hi, guys," he said breezily. "What's new with his Majesty?"

"It's in Hong Kong," Joe said.

Chet shook his head when he heard the story. "Tough break," he said. Then he turned to Aunt Gertrude. "You haven't signed my cast. Tell you what. I'll let you autograph it in exchange for a piece of pie."

He offered a pen to Miss Hardy. She signed her name on the white surface, which by now had been crisscrossed by other signatures. "There," she said. "If it weren't for that Ruby King and those cutthroats connected with it, you wouldn't have broken your arm."

"It's all in the line of duty," Chet said with a grin. "Anything for my friends."

At that moment the doorbell rang. Frank answered it. Outside stood a man who introduced himself as Peter Carpenter and presented credentials indicating that he was from the security section of the International Insurance Company.

"I'd like to speak to Fenton Hardy," he said.

"He's not here at the moment," Frank told him. "But won't you come in? Maybe my brother Joe and I can help you. I'm Frank Hardy."

"I've heard of you," Carpenter said. "Yes, I'll talk to you."

Frank led the visitor into the living room where Mrs. Hardy, Aunt Gertrude, and Joe joined them. Chet lingered in the kitchen over a slab of peach pie with an ear cocked to the living room.

"We would like either your father or you to accept an assignment for us," the man began.

"Sorry, but we're busy on something else. So is our father," Frank said.

"You mean the Ruby King?"

"How did you know?"

"That's the case I'm referring to. It was insured with us." Carpenter produced a file and went on, "My company stands to pay a sizable settlement unless the chess piece is found. We want you to find it!"

"Mr. Krassner asked us to do the same thing," Joe said. "Unfortunately we have reason to believe that the Ruby King has been shipped out of the country. It might be in Hong Kong."

"Then you must fly to Hong Kong immediately!"

# CHAPTER XVI

## *A Bold Caper*

"Your father could join you once your preliminary investigation is underway," Mr. Carpenter continued. "Your age also is in your favor. You can pose as students or tourists."

Frank and Joe were dumfounded! They tried to take the proposal calmly, but their hearts raced with excitement at the prospect of a trip to the Orient.

"We'll talk it over with Dad," Frank said. "How can we get in touch with you, Mr. Carpenter?"

"I'll be in my office until tomorrow afternoon, and I do hope you'll accept the assignment. All expenses paid and a fee based upon a percentage of the money you save us."

Seconds after the man left, Chet burst into the living room. "What's going on?" he asked. "Did I hear that man say something about going to Hong Kong?"

"You did," Aunt Gertrude said. "And the answer is no!"

"Now, Gertrude," Mrs. Hardy said, "it might not be such a bad idea."

"Bad! It'll be a calamity! We'll never see these boys again. They might be kidnapped and taken to an opium den!"

"Don't worry about a thing," Chet spoke up. "With me to help them they'll be perfectly safe!"

"Chet, you've got a broken arm," Joe said. "You couldn't help."

"What do you mean? I can really conk someone with this cast!"

"Look, old buddy," Frank said, and put an arm around his friend's shoulder. "The insurance company will only pay for our expenses, not yours."

"I've got a couple of dollars," Chet said. "And besides, I like Chinese food!"

"*No!*" Joe said.

"Aw, shucks!" Chet tried to smile as he left the Hardy house. "Will you bring me a souvenir at least? Like a carved dagger?"

"Too dangerous," Frank replied. "How about an incense burner?"

"Phooey!" Chet said, and a minute later his car sputtered off.

Frank and Joe contacted the airport. There were no flights available until two days later, and that plane would leave early in the morning.

"I'm sure Dad'll go along with the idea," Joe

said. "Let's get passports and our inoculation shots right away."

"Good. Then we'll visit Mrs. Krassner. Maybe she'll give us a letter of introduction to her family."

Tingling with excitement, Frank and Joe drove first to the doctor for the necessary shots, then to the banker's estate where Mrs. Krassner received them cordially. Her husband was at his office. When she heard that they planned to go to Hong Kong, the Chinese woman's eyebrows raised. "You don't think it would be too dangerous?"

"We've handled risky assignments before," Frank assured her. "Could we meet your family, Mrs. Krassner?"

"I'm sure they'd be delighted to help you in any way. Are you certain the Ruby King was taken there?"

"Reasonably certain," Frank said.

Mrs. Krassner went into the library, where she penned a note in Chinese. "Give this to my father, Moy Chen-Chin," she said.

"Any directions?" Joe asked.

Mrs. Krassner smiled. "Everybody knows Moy Chen-Chin."

On the way home the young detectives exulted over this rare opportunity. "Should we tell Conrad Greene about this tonight?" Joe asked.

"Sure. Why not? After the exhibition," Frank said.

At dinner that night Mrs. Hardy said, "Boys, where are your appetites? You're just picking at your food."

"I guess we're too excited," Frank said. "Hurry up, Joe. The chess exhibition starts soon."

The VFW hall, a barnlike auditorium, with wooden folding chairs, was half-filled when the Hardys arrived. On the stage was a long table, where six of Conrad Greene's opponents were already seated.

"Conrad will probably come through the back door," Joe said. "He's not one to rub elbows with the peasantry."

The boys looked about, nodding here and there to friends and neighbors. Suddenly a scuffling sounded from backstage.

"Help! Help!" a man screamed.

"That's Conrad!" Frank cried out.

The Hardys ran forward and vaulted onto the stage. There was a door on either side. Joe took the left, Frank the right. The room behind was empty! They raced out the back door and looked around. Nobody was there but a boy of about ten.

"I saw him!" the boy volunteered. "I saw everything!"

"Tell us what happened. Hurry!" Joe urged.

The youngster said he was parking his bicycle when he noticed a man enter the building.

"Then two guys jumped from a car and pounced on him. I saw it right through the door there. The man screamed and kicked, but the two bad guys dragged him to the car."

"Where'd they go?" Frank asked.

The boy indicated a side street, which led to the dock area.

Frank and Joe thanked the boy and hurried to a nearby telephone booth, where they called police headquarters. Collig was off duty, but a lieutenant took the report that Conrad Greene had been kidnapped. He said he would dispatch a car to the VFW Hall to check out the incident.

After he hung up, Joe said, "Frank, maybe they took Greene to the *Queen Maru!* I still think Ono's in with the serpent gang!"

"The ship's not due to sail until midnight," Frank said. "We'll have a little time. Let's go down to the dock."

They were just pulling up to the pier when Frank cried out, "Hey! Look!"

The *Queen Maru* was moving slowly away from her berth!

"She's leaving ahead of time," Joe said. "Come on, Frank. We've got to stop them!"

The boys called headquarters again. Chief Collig had been notified and was there busily organizing a search for the kidnapped man.

"We think he's on the *Queen Maru!*" Frank said. "She's sailing ahead of schedule."

"Good work, boys," the chief said. "I'll send the police launch to intercept them."

"We'll go in the *Sleuth*," Frank said. "Meet you out in the bay!"

The Hardys' sleek speedboat was berthed three blocks away. The boys ran to the boathouse and in minutes were streaking across Barmet Bay, their powerful searchlight skimming over the wave tops.

In a few minutes the gray hulk of the *Queen Maru* loomed on the dark horizon. Joe was at the wheel of the *Sleuth* and circled the slow-moving cargo ship.

"There's not a soul on deck," Frank remarked.

He looked back toward the harbor. The *Queen*, despite her lumbering pace, was putting more and more distance between Bayport and the open sea. Near the three-mile limit, the boys spied a light racing toward them from a distance.

"Here comes the launch," Frank said.

The police boat approached with signal lights blinking. The message was easily translated by the Hardys. "Police. Stop immediately!"

Seconds later the lights blinked again. "Lower a ladder. We are boarding."

The launch pulled alongside the freighter. Three officers scrambled up to the deck. Frank and Joe latched the *Sleuth* onto the launch and climbed up behind them.

The party was met by Captain Ono, his face wreathed in a broad smile.

"What can I do for you now?" he asked, fixing the Hardys with a long look.

"There's been a kidnapping," Chief Collig said. "We think the victim may be on your ship."

Ono bowed. "Go ahead and search. I have neither a box nor a prisoner."

The police began a careful search of the holds, galley, crews' quarters, and the captain's cabin as well. Meanwhile, Frank and Joe sauntered over the deck.

"Let's check the lifeboats," Frank suggested.

They looked beneath the canvas cover of each one, but could see nothing suspicious. Just as the police emerged from the holds, they approached the last lifeboat.

At one end of it, the sea breeze fluttered a piece of the covering which had come loose.

"Watch it, Joe," Frank warned. "It might not have been the wind that tore off the canvas!" He signaled Chief Collig. "Over here!" he called.

The officers ran to the lifeboat. One flashed his light under the canvas, then barked a crisp order. "Come out with your hands up!"

The cowering figure of a man emerged above the gunwale.

"Holy crow!" Joe exclaimed. "It's Gerard Henry!"

## CHAPTER XVII

## *The Chinese Note*

THE prisoner looked surly as the police pulled him to the deck and snapped on handcuffs. Captain Ono, who came running up, was flabbergasted.

"Is—is this your kidnapped man?" he asked.

"No," Collig replied. "But he's an escaped felon."

"How did you get on my ship?" Ono asked Henry sternly.

The man confessed that he had climbed a rope and reached the deck shortly before the *Queen* sailed. Collig turned to Ono. "Why did you leave ahead of schedule?"

"All was in readiness. So why wait?"

"Did you notify the harbor master?"

"Of course. We adhere to proper procedure."

The prisoner was led down to the police launch

and Ono was told he could proceed. Frank and Joe hopped into the *Sleuth* and headed home.

When they arrived they received a phone call from their father. Frank answered it. He told about their proposed trip to Hong Kong and asked, "Is it okay with you, Dad?"

"Sure. I'll follow you as soon as I can. Right now I'm going to Dallas. Seems a branch of the tailoring-jewelry racket has sprung up there."

The next morning at breakfast there was a knock on the back door and Phil Cohen entered.

"Hi, Phil," Frank said. "What brings you over here so early?"

Phil looked serious. "I noticed something funny and wanted to talk to you. It's about Chet."

"What about him?"

"He went into Paul Goo's Chinese Laundry yesterday afternoon."

"Nothing funny about that," Joe said. "Maybe he took his shirts."

"You know his mother does all his laundry. He took nothing and picked nothing up. Before he went in he glanced up and down the street as if he wanted to make sure no one saw him. It looked suspicious to me."

"Hm!" Frank said thoughtfully. "Why would he do that?"

"That's just it. It's not like Chet," Phil said. "Maybe he got mixed up in your Chinese mystery somehow, being that he spends so much time with Krassner—"

"I'll get to the bottom of this right now," Frank broke in. He picked up the telephone and dialed the Morton farm. Chet answered.

"Hey, old buddy," Frank said, "what were you doing in Paul Goo's laundry yesterday?"

There was silence on the other end. Then Chet said, "Who told you?"

"A little Chinese bird. What were you doing there?"

"Nothing much. Just got some lechee nuts."

"Tell me the truth, Chet!"

"I am. Is it against the law to visit a Chinese laundry?" Chet would say nothing more.

When he hung up, Frank felt uneasy. "Let's check out the laundry," he suggested.

"Right," Joe agreed. "But first we'd better stop at headquarters. Maybe there's some news on Conrad."

"See you later," Phil said. "Let me know what develops." He left through the back door when giggling voices of girls could be heard in the front. After a brief knock, Joe opened the door and Callie Shaw and Iola Morton breezed in.

Frank grinned at Callie, a pretty blond girl with brown eyes, whom he often dated. "Hi. What's up?"

"We're selling tickets to a benefit."

"When, where, why?"

"Tonight in our barn," Iola said. "Eight o'clock sharp."

"But for whose benefit?" Joe inquired.

"That's our secret. You're coming, of course." Iola reached into her pocket and pulled out two tickets. She handed them to Joe. "You can pay us later," she said.

Just then Mrs. Hardy and Aunt Gertrude came in and greeted the girls. As they chatted, the boys drove off to headquarters. There they learned two pertinent facts. Nothing had been heard from Conrad Greene, and they were told that Paul Goo, the Chinese laundry owner, had an impeccable reputation.

"He's been in this country a long time," Chief Collig said. "A friendly old duck. Likes kids."

Frank and Joe thanked the officer, then drove to Mully Street. It was the main thoroughfare of Bayport's Little Chinatown. They passed two restaurants, a Chinese grocery, and a gift shop before coming to Paul Goo's place. They parked and went in. A tinkling bell announced their presence. The interior of the shop smelled of soap, starch, and steam.

Behind an ironing board stood Paul Goo, a spare, elderly man, whose eyes were shuttered in deep fleshy folds. "Hello," he said with a smile. "You have some shirts?"

"Not today," Frank said. "We want to ask your prices."

"Oh yes. Very reasonable here." Goo handed the boy a small printed paper listing his services.

"Thank you," Frank said. "Do you have lechee nuts?"

The elderly man blinked. "Sure. For my friends." He put a hand beneath the counter, produced two of the thin-shelled nuts so popular with Orientals, and handed one to each boy.

"Thank you," Joe said. "You are very kind."

They turned to go, but Frank hesitated a moment. "Are you from Hong Kong, Mr. Goo?"

The laundryman smiled broadly. "Yes. How you guess? Most people in Little Chinatown are from Hong Kong."

Outside, the boys cracked the nuts. "Not bad," Joe said. "What do you think of Goo, Frank?"

"He seems all right. But you never can tell. Let's put a tail on good old Chet and find out what's going on."

Joe snapped his fingers. "Phil Cohen would be a good man for the job!"

The Hardys stopped at Phil's home. The sound of piano playing drifted across the front lawn and the boys found their friend busily composing a song.

"Sorry to disturb your symphony," Joe said, "but do you have time for a surveillance job?"

"I think so. What is it?"

"Follow Chet. See if he goes to that Chinese laundry again. He may be headed for trouble."

"Will do," Phil agreed. "I'll phone Iola. She can tell me when Chet's coming into town again."

"Thanks, pal," Frank said.

As Frank and Joe drove off, they heard Phil picking on the piano keys again. An hour later he called them at home.

"I spoke to Iola, and guess what? Chet's on his way to town!" he reported. "I'm going to Mully Street right away."

"Good. Keep out of sight and let us know what's happening."

While the Hardys ate lunch, Phil hurried off to Mully Street. He stationed himself in a doorway where he had Paul Goo's shop in a clear line of sight. And he did not have to wait long.

Down the street strolled Chet, his lips moving as if he were mumbling to himself.

"The poor guy's gone bananas," Phil thought. He left his hiding place and quietly fell in behind Chet, who seemed oblivious to the whole world.

When he stepped into the laundry, Phil flattened himself against the building and listened. He could not make out any words, but Chet and Goo conversed for about ten minutes in low tones. Then another customer entered. The mumbling ceased and Chet came out, a piece of paper in his hand.

His eyes were so intent upon it that he bumped squarely into Phil. "Oh, hello there," he said.

"Getting more nuts?" Phil asked.

Chet was not the least shaken by the point-blank query. "No. Not today. Well, I have to go now."

Phil watched Chet walk away. Suddenly he noticed the piece of paper fall to the ground. Unaware of it, Chet got into his jalopy and drove off.

Phil ran to the spot and picked it up. His eyes widened in surprise. "Wait till the Hardys see this!" he said to himself. Minutes later he drove up to their home.

"Hey, Frank, Joe!" he called out as he rushed to the door.

"What's the matter?" Frank let him in. "You're all out of breath."

"Look at this!" Phil handed him the paper.

On it were lines of Chinese characters, delicately brush-stroked. Alongside each were phonetic pronunciations written in English.

Joe said, "Maybe Chet's some kind of go-between. It could be a message!"

"And he might have to deliver it orally, hence the mumbling," Phil remarked, and relayed the information he had gleaned on his surveillance.

"We'll have to take this to an Oriental language expert," Frank said.

"You do that," Phil said. "I'll get back to my song."

He left, and while Frank and Joe were studying the mysterious paper, the telephone rang. Joe answered. It was Conrad Greene's father.

*Phil flattened himself against the building and listened.*

"I have some information for you," he said in a quavering voice.

"What is it?"

"I can't tell you on the phone. Come over here as soon as you can!"

"What a day," Joe said to Frank with a sigh. "Mr. Greene wants to see us pronto. Do you suppose he received a ransom demand?"

"We'll find out soon. Come on."

The boys went to their car after quickly telling their mother where they were headed. Forty-five minutes later they parked in front of the house on the cliff. They hastened to the door and were flabbergasted when it was opened by the grand-master himself!

"Conrad Greene!" Frank exclaimed. "How did you get loose? Where were you held? Who kidnapped you?"

"Come in and I'll answer your questions one at a time," Greene said with a grin.

In the living room his story unfolded. He had not seen his captors, because a hood had been clapped over his head. Where he was held was a mystery, too, but the why was perfectly clear.

"My captors warned me not to win the international championship!" he said. "They didn't hurt me, but guaranteed that I would be if I made an attempt to win. They drove me back just a little while ago."

"Have you notified the police?" Frank asked.

"Not yet. I wanted to tell you first."

Frank grabbed the phone and spoke to Chief Collig. Then he said, "Come on, Joe. We'll disconnect that phone tap. I don't think the gang is being fooled by it any longer, if they ever were."

The job was quickly accomplished, and as Joe climbed down from the pole, a police car drove up. It was Lieutenant Skillman from the Ocean Bluffs force.

"Chief Collig notified me," he said. "He also got in touch with the FBI. I'm sure they'll have a lot of questions for Mr. Greene."

The boys left as Conrad beckoned Skillman into the house. On the way home, Frank said, "I think this whole caper was done to unnerve Conrad."

"No doubt," Joe agreed.

They mulled over the latest developments. The serpent gang had carried off the Ruby King, and it seemed logical that they also had been the ones who had kidnapped Greene. But why did they want him to lose the championship, now that he could not receive the valuable prize, anyway?

"It just doesn't make sense," Frank said.

"Well, what do we do next?" Joe asked.

Frank looked at his watch. "It's too late to have that Chinese note deciphered now. We'll just be in time for dinner. And the party starts at eight."

When the Hardys reached the Morton farm, the barn behind the house was vibrating with music. Frank and Joe entered to find the place festooned with colorful crepe paper and balloons. They recognized many of their friends from high school and the Bayport area. Couples were dancing to the rhythmic tunes produced by a three-piece combo.

"Wow, what a blast!" Joe said.

When Callie and Iola noticed the boys, they came over, took them by the hand, and led them to a long table. On it stood a punch bowl and a variety of sandwiches.

"Now tell us what this is all about, Iola," Joe urged. "You said the party was for a benefit?"

"Right. Yours, to be exact."

"Wait a minute. What—?"

Iola interrupted him by putting a hand on his arm. At the same time she tapped a spoon on the punch bowl and called out, "Silence, please!"

Everyone became quiet.

"As you all know," Iola began, "our two private eyes are going to Hong Kong on a most dangerous mission. We, their friends, felt they needed a bodyguard—a big one. We are holding this party to raise extra money for that bodyguard."

The Hardys were dumfounded. "Who is he?" Joe finally asked.

"Who else?" Chet declared, a grin on his face.

Everyone cheered.

"We should have guessed," Joe said. "He *is* the biggest one of our friends—or rather the fattest!"

"But size alone is not enough," Chet said. "I have made myself indispensable in other ways!"

"Such as?" Frank had a hard time keeping a straight face.

"I learned Chinese! Listen: Ho-La-Ma, Mmm Goy, Ngor But Duck Lew Ah-h-h, Gau Miang Ah-h-h, Mau Sot Ah-h-h-h!"

"Those were the words on the paper!" Frank said.

Chet's lips curled in a supercilious smile. "Of course. My gag worked. I dropped it on purpose."

Frank and Joe slapped Chet on the back. "Now tell us what all that means!" Joe asked.

Chet took a deep breath. "Hello—please, I'm in trouble—help—murder!"

# CHAPTER XVIII

## *Kim-Kim*

AT a signal from Phil Cohen, the combo broke out in a catchy tune. Everyone started to sing:

> Frank, Joe, and Chet, farewell to thee,
> Sock 'em, rock 'em
> Till the Ruby King is free.
> Hello, Hong Kong,
> You can't hide Fong
> or the slippery Eggleby.

Joe laughed at the serenade, and Frank recognized the tune Phil had been composing on his piano. Then came a rousing refrain:

> For the Hardys will get you
> Sooner or later,
> So surrender right now while you can.
> They'll give you fits
> With their uncanny wits.
> They always come up with their man!

The merrymaking still rang in the minds of Frank, Joe, and sleepy-eyed Chet when they set off from Bayport at six o'clock the next morning. After the first two transfers the flight became monotonous and the boys were weary by the time the big plane landed in heavy rain at Kai Tak Airport the following evening. They retrieved their baggage, then went through customs.

"Before we leave the airport," Frank said, "let's check on the rug."

They made their way to the freight terminal and inquired about the shipment. The clerk told them he did not know the name of the man who had picked up the rug but would check it out and call them at the hotel.

"Thank you," Frank said and they left. Outside the terminal they hailed a taxi and gave the driver the address of their hotel, the Star Terminal, in Kowloon.

As they approached the city, Chet said, "Wow, this is a big place!"

"What did you expect?" Frank needled. "A dreamy little fishing village? Take a look across the bay!"

Part way up the Hong Kong hill, white high-rise apartments rose like sentinels, looking down on modern glass-and-steel office buildings in the harbor area.

Finally they arrived at their destination. "Boy, I'm beat," Chet complained.

"We'll hit the sack as soon as we get upstairs," Joe said.

They checked in and half an hour later were sound asleep.

The next morning they woke up refreshed and excited by prospects of adventure in the Orient. Joe pulled open the curtains. "Hey, take in that view!" he said, pointing to ferryboats plying their way back and forth in the harbor among the many junks, sampans, and small fishing boats.

"Give me breakfast before any view," Chet said.

"Not a bad idea," Frank agreed. "After we eat we'll go to visit Mrs. Krassner's parents. I'll call them right now and tell them we're coming."

An hour later the boys hastened down to the ferry slip to await the next boat to Hong Kong. They joined the good-natured, jostling crowd that elbowed onto the craft like a colony of ants.

Frank, Joe, and Chet sat on the upper deck and watched as the teeming shore of Hong Kong came closer and closer. The ferry glided smoothly into its slip and the three debarked.

Frank hailed a taxi and told the Chinese driver to take them to Moy Chen-Chin's house.

"Ah, so." The man nodded and smiled, obviously impressed with the importance of his riders.

The higher the road snaked up the hill, the more luxurious the homes became. Finally they reached the estate of Moy Chen-Chin and were amazed by its opulence.

Formal gardens bordered both sides of the drive and gave the grounds the appearance of a royal park. Men were trimming, pruning, and tending the flower beds.

The taxi stopped in front of a beautiful house with a wide terrace. An elderly couple came out to meet them and introduced themselves as Mr. and Mrs. Moy.

As they led the boys to the veranda, Chet whispered to Frank, "I thought their name was Chin."

"In Chinese the last name always comes first," Frank replied.

As soon as tea was served, the Moys plied the boys with questions about their daughter Mrs. Krassner and her husband.

After the Americans had told them all about Bayport and their life at home, Mr. Moy said seriously, "We know you have come for the Ruby King. Will you take some advice from a wise old man?"

"What is it?" Frank asked.

"Drop your case. It will bring you only misery, even death!"

The awkward silence that followed was broken by Chet, who said *"Daw Jer"* which meant "Thank you."

Mrs. Moy smiled. "Oh, you speak our language. Where did you learn it?"

"At Paul Goo's laundry," Chet said and told his story, which the Chinese couple found very amusing.

"You must see all the sights," Mr. Moy said.

"Spend a week or two and have a good vacation. Then return home."

"We'll tour the area to get our bearings," Frank said. "But really, Mr. Moy, we can't take your advice. We have an obligation to Mr. Krassner and the insurance company which is paying for our trip."

Mr. Moy shrugged slightly. Then he said, "Our chauffeur Daniel will take you on a tour. Shall I send him to the hotel tomorrow, say, at ten o'clock?"

"That would be great!" Joe said.

A few minutes later the boys thanked the cordial couple and went back to their hotel. On the way Frank said, "I wonder why Mr. Moy made that remark about the Ruby King. He sounds like Conrad Greene's father!"

"He must know about the curse, too," Joe said.

At the hotel they found a message from the airport. The name of the man who had picked up the rug was Choy Bok. But there was no address.

"Let's look in the telephone book," Joe suggested.

After thumbing through the directory he was perplexed. "Six people are listed under that name," he said.

"We'd better check out each one," Frank said.

"I don't know if that's such a good idea," Joe countered. "We may tip off the real Choy Bok in the process."

"I'm aware of that," his brother replied. "But we have to start somewhere. If any of these men react to the password *Shah mat*, at least it will give us a lead."

The boys left the hotel again, hired a taxi, and were on their way. The first two Choy Boks lived in the poorest section of town, and neither spoke English. The driver acted as an interpreter while Frank talked to the men. They looked blank when he mentioned the password, and the Hardys were convinced that they were not involved with the serpent gang.

The young detectives were no luckier with the next three, who were also poor, elderly men. The last Choy Bok lived in a high-rise apartment, seemed reasonably well-to-do, and spoke good English.

He greeted the boys affably, and when Frank mentioned the password, he said, "Oh, you play chess?"

Frank nodded. "We have a chess club in Bayport, where we come from. One of the members is Chinese. Told us to visit his friend Choy Bok in Hong Kong."

"Oh? What's your friend's name?"

"Fong," Frank said. He watched the man intently.

Choy Bok raised his eyebrows. "I don't think I know him."

"Well, he forgot to give us the address. We

looked in the phone book, but must have made a mistake."

"I think you did. But have a cup of tea, anyway."

Mr. Choy called his wife and the friendly couple served them a snack. They talked amiably to the Americans for quite some time, then Frank rose. The boys thanked the Choys and left.

Tired and discouraged from the long day's sleuthing, they returned to their hotel.

As they trudged up to their room, Joe said, "I'm afraid the whole thing was for the birds. I'm sure none of the men we talked to is a member of the Serpents."

Frank nodded. "I'm inclined to agree. Whoever comes up with a good idea on what to do next gets a prize."

"Let's have dinner and call it a day," Chet said. "And I'll take the prize."

"That kind of idea doesn't qualify," Frank said. "But we'll follow your advice."

The next morning at ten o'clock sharp Mr. Moy's chauffeur arrived. "I'll take you through town and out to Aberdeen," he said. "Then if we have time, to the New Territories, which overlook the Peoples' Republic of China."

For many miles the road led along a barren shoreline. Then they came to a bay with hundreds of sampans lying side by side.

"Do people live on the water like this?" Chet asked.

Daniel, the driver, nodded. "This is Aberdeen. The government is trying to get the sampan dwellers to move into new developments, but their way of life is hard to change." He stopped for a few minutes while the boys took photographs with a palm-size camera Frank and Joe had brought along.

As they clicked away, a small boy climbed up a steep embankment to the road. "Me Kim-Kim. I help you," he said.

"I don't think we need you," Frank replied, but the ten-year-old was not to be deterred.

He attached himself to Chet. "I help *you!*" he said. "You big man. I carry your camera."

Kim-Kim wore tattered shorts and a discarded army jacket, its long sleeves hanging down over his hands. As the Americans returned to the car, he slipped in beside Chet before anyone could stop him.

"Out!" Daniel commanded.

But Kim-Kim refused. He kicked and struggled, and clung to Chet's neck.

"Okay," Frank said. "We'll take him back with us, give him a square meal, and turn him over to the police."

The little fellow grinned. "I bring you good luck!" he promised.

After Daniel had been driving a while, Frank

noticed a semicircular wall built into a hillside. He asked about it.

"It's an armchair grave," Daniel replied. He explained that the deceased were buried in such graves for one year. Then their bones were disinterred and placed in earthen jars. He pointed. "There's one now."

In a farm field stood a mud-colored container about three feet high.

"It looks like my mother's cookie jar," Chet commented.

"A little gruesome, isn't it?" Joe said.

Then suddenly the monsoon rains hit. Water came down in torrents and the road ahead of them turned into a river.

"This could be dangerous," Daniel said, and turned the car around.

Traffic moved along slowly. As they edged past the hillside, a wall of mud slid down, nearly blocking the road. But Daniel drove skillfully over the sheet of yellow slime, finally guiding the car safely back to Kowloon.

"So that's a monsoon!" Chet said as they entered the hotel.

"Well, Kim-Kim, you got us through that," Joe said, opening the door to their room. "And now into the shower with you!"

By dinnertime Kim-Kim, who said he was an orphan, had convinced the boys to let him stay with them as an interpreter as long as they were in Hong Kong. After breakfast the next day, while Chet bought him some new clothes, Frank read about the storm in the morning English newspaper.

"Hey, look at this!" he said suddenly. "Ming Do's obituary!"

The world-famous collector of chess pieces had died two days before. The funeral was to take place the next afternoon. The article said that Ming Do was the oldest member of the Royal Chess Club of Hong Kong.

"Ming Do!" Joe exclaimed. "That cable we found mentioned that a man by that name was very ill!"

"Right. He must have been the customer who wanted the Ruby King!" Frank said.

They told Chet the news when he returned. "Wow!" he said. "Who's going to buy it now?"

Frank shrugged. "Maybe we can learn something at the Royal Chess Club."

They discussed strategy. Chet and Kim-Kim would stay outside the club, which was located not far from their hotel. The Hardys would go in and investigate.

Frank and Joe entered the plush interior thirty minutes later and looked about. A chill of recognition ran down Joe's spine. He nudged his brother.

Sitting at a table at the far end corner was Fong, playing chess with another man!

The Hardys approached as close as they could without being seen. Then they slipped behind a heavy drapery to eavesdrop.

The men talked in low tones, and the name Ruby King could be heard now and then.

"Who do you suppose that other guy is?" Joe asked.

Suddenly the Hardys became aware of a commotion. They peered from their hiding place to see Kim-Kim running into the club with Chet chasing him!

"Frank, Joe!" Kim-Kim cried out.

"Good grief," Frank said. "Now we're in trouble!"

# CHAPTER XIX

## *The Payoff*

"Come here, Kim-Kim! Wait!" Chet called as surprised club members looked askance at the intruders.

But the small Chinese boy did not stop. His sharp eyes searched the room until they alighted upon the feet of Frank and Joe showing beneath the drapery. He revealed their hiding place, took both by the hand, and pulled the embarrassed Hardys out into the room.

"What are you doing?" Joe muttered.

"No time to lose!" Kim-Kim said. "Big danger!"

His eyes glinting with anger, Fong rose from his chessboard and confronted the eavesdroppers. He beckoned two attendants and spat out some Chinese, whereupon the men grasped the boys by the arms.

"So! The detective babies have left the Bayport playpen. How quaint! What do you want here?"

"You know!" Joe shot back. "You and your crooked Serpents!"

Fong laughed derisively and the men standing about smiled at the discomfiture of the young Americans. "Play your children's games somewhere else," Fong went on. "But I warn you both —and your fat friend, too—you are not in the United States now. Go home before it's too late!"

He spoke more Chinese to the attendants, who promptly hustled the boys and Kim-Kim out into the street. When the bouncers had disappeared, Frank said, "Chet, for heaven's sake, why did you let Kim-Kim blow our cover?"

"I didn't mean to," Chet apologized. "He heard something you should know about, and before I could tell him to wait, he ran in there."

"What is it?"

Kim-Kim turned his head slowly and said in a whisper, "Those two men across the street—in front of store window—no look now—they going to kill you. Say so in Chinese!"

"Okay, Kim-Kim, don't worry about it. We'll take care of it," Joe said, trying to calm the excited child.

The Hardys engaged in casual chatter while Frank took out the tiny camera and unobtrusively snapped a few pictures of the men. Then they walked toward the hotel and stopped at a camera shop to drop off the film. Prints were promised that evening.

"We might never see them," Chet said pessimistically. "I'll bet someone followed us."

"Those two guys didn't, I made sure of that," Joe replied. "Anyway, it might help to learn who they are. If they're really out to get us, maybe the police could arrest them."

Back at the hotel, Chet and Kim-Kim remained in the lobby coffee shop while the Hardys took the elevator to their room. Joe turned the key in the lock and pushed open the door.

There sat Fong, smiling like a welcome guest, his feet resting on a coffee table! "Surprise!" he said.

"How did you get in?" Joe demanded angrily.

"Calm down," Fong said, and beckoned the Hardys to be seated. "How I got in is simple enough. Kowloon is my turf, as you say in the States."

"What do you want?" Frank asked. "You've got the Ruby King!"

"Money. I want money," Fong replied. "You can get it for me and save your necks at the same time. Sound interesting?"

"What do you mean?" Joe asked.

Fong removed his feet and leaned forward intently, gesturing with his long, slender hands. "I will sell the Ruby King to the insurance company you represent," Fong said, "at a depressed figure

—say twenty-five thousand dollars. The claim will cost them much more than that."

Frank's mind whirled. Of course the serpent gang must have deduced that their trip to Hong Kong was paid by the insurance company who had to pay for the loss of the King. What a cunning plan!

"And what if they don't accept this offer?"

"They will," Fong said. "It's smart business. Phone me at the chess club when you get a reply from your employer." He rose, went to the door, and turned around. This time his face had a sinister expression.

"By the way, no police involvement, or Mrs. Krassner's family will be in big trouble!"

A sudden thought flashed through Frank's mind. "Is that how you got her to leave her husband's safe open?"

The question seemed to jolt Fong but only for a split second. "Let's say Mrs. Krassner could be persuaded," he said unctuously. "She knows the power of the Serpents. You should follow her example."

When Fong had left, the boys discussed the strange offer and Mrs. Krassner's part in the disappearance of the chess piece.

"I feel sorry for her," Joe said.

Just then running footsteps sounded in the hall and Chet flung open the door with a bang. Kim-Kim stood, wild-eyed, beside him.

"F-Fong!" Chet said. "He just came off the elevator. I thought maybe he—"

"Had murdered us?" Joe said.

"Yes. I'm sure glad to see you alive."

Joe told Chet what had happened, while Frank composed a message to the insurance company. Then they went downstairs to the desk and sent the cable.

For the balance of the day and through the dinner hour, the Hardys speculated on the outcome of Fong's proposal. Whatever the decision of the insurance company, the boys faced considerable risk.

If the answer was "no deal," their lives certainly would be in jeopardy. Even if the money were sent, there was no telling whether the Serpents would carry out their end of the bargain.

As Chet put it, "Fong might take the twenty-five thousand dollars and keep the Ruby King too. Then what would you do?"

"It wouldn't make any difference," Joe said, "because we probably wouldn't be alive to tell the tale."

Leaving Chet and his Oriental shadow to linger over dessert, Frank and Joe stepped out into the muggy night air and made sure they were not being followed as they walked to the photography shop. The prints were waiting and the Hardys examined them.

"Good clear shots," Joe said. "What next?"

"Let's take them to the police," Frank said. "Maybe we can find out who our charming friends are."

At headquarters the captain in charge, a tall, thin fellow named Hawkins, identified the two men instantly. "They're hit men for the serpent mob," he said.

"A friend of ours heard them say they'll kill us," Frank said.

"Then my advice is to be very careful. Unfortunately this is not enough to press charges and to arrest them. We've been trying to crack that ring for a long time, but without success."

In their hotel again, the three boys and Kim-Kim studied the inscrutable faces of the hit men. "I've a hunch we'll see them again," Joe said.

They were all at breakfast the next morning when a cablegram was delivered for the Hardys by a bellhop. Frank took the envelope and opened it. "From International Insurance," he said. "They accepted the offer!" The message said twenty-five thousand dollars had already been deposited in a Hong Kong bank.

The Hardys were to take it out in cash and buy the Ruby King back. The cable ended, "As much as we dislike this arrangement, it seems feasible at this time. Please be extremely cautious."

The boys hastily finished their meal and telephoned the chess club. Fong was not there and they left a message for him to return the call.

Only ten minutes elapsed before he telephoned.

"Fong speaking. What's the deal?"

"Affirmative," Frank said.

"Ah, good. It will be a cash transaction."

"Of course."

"And no police!"

"They haven't been told," Frank said.

"Then here's how we'll do it," Fong said. "Got a pencil and paper?"

"Yes. Go ahead."

Fong spoke slowly while Frank took notes. After the Hardys obtained the cash they were to take a taxi out past Aberdeen and into the countryside. "That Chinese kid with you will show you the way," the man said.

He then mentioned a small settlement of sampans. One mile to the north, on the right-hand side of the road, they would see a bone jar one hundred and fifty yards from a farmer's shack made of corrugated sheet metal.

"You understand what a bone jar is?" Fong asked.

"Yes. I've seen one."

"Put the cash in it. It's empty."

"What about the Ruby King?" Frank asked.

"A note in the jar will tell you where to find it."

The time was set for twelve-thirty that afternoon, and before Fong hung up, he warned that any double cross would be fatal.

The young detectives were keyed up with almost unbearable excitement. They hastened to the bank, where the manager frowned in disbelief as he counted out the amount in large bills and tied the money in a small package. Joe put it inside his shirt and they returned to the hotel.

"Whew!" Frank said, rubbing the sweat from the palms of his hands. "So far so good."

Carefully following Fong's directions, the four set off by taxi toward the rendezvous. Kim-Kim looked wistfully at the city of junks and sampans as they passed by Aberdeen. All watched for the hut and the bone jar.

"There it is," Chet finally said, pointing to the side of the road.

"Looks like it all right," Frank agreed. "Stop here, driver."

They got out and walked toward the dun-colored jar. Two farmers, sharpening sickles, watched from the side of the tin shack. Nearing the jar, Chet tripped over a bundle of bamboo poles lying in the tall grass.

"Careful. Don't break your other arm," Joe said.

All this time Kim-Kim kept his eyes on the two men. "They no look happy," he said.

"They probably work for the Serpents," Joe remarked, "and are disguised as farmers."

"No," Kim-Kim said. "They real farmers and they get madder."

The boys had reached the bone jar and Frank

boldly removed the lid. He put his hand inside. "Let's get the directions to the Ruby King first," he said, feeling about until his fingers touched something soft and at the same time hard.

*Frank pulled out a fistful of matted hair and bones!*

"Ugh!" he said in disgust. "Somebody's remains are in here!"

"Yes. I think so too," Kim-Kim said. "Here come farmers. Very mad."

The two men raced toward the trespassers brandishing the sickles, which gleamed in the midday sunshine.

"Holy crow!" Joe exclaimed. "Maybe it's the wrong bone jar!"

"Either that, or it's a booby trap!" Frank said. "Run!"

The boys ran toward the waiting taxi, but Chet, with his arm in the cast, could not keep up.

"Hey, don't let 'em chop me up!" he pleaded.

Frank and Joe stopped to pick up the bamboo poles, and when the irate farmers approached, they warded off the sickle blows, while Kim-Kim ardently apologized in Chinese.

But the enraged farmers could not be mollified. One of them flung his weapon and it came at Frank's head like a spinning boomerang!

# CHAPTER XX

## *The Beggars of Tai Pak*

"Duck!" Joe's warning sent Frank tumbling into grass, and the sickle sailed harmlessly over him. He regained his feet to see the farmers standing with arms akimbo, glowering at the retreating intruders.

Panting for breath, the boys reached the taxi and piled in on top of one another. When the door slammed shut, the driver sped off and Kim-Kim climbed into the front seat. He grinned back at the Americans.

"Farmers very mad. You disturbed honorable ancestors!"

"We didn't mean to. How did we ever get the wrong place?" Joe wondered.

"I'll tell you how," Frank said. "Look up ahead. There's another shack and another bone jar. This must be it!"

"Please, fellows," Chet begged, "be more careful this time. I'm not quite ready to be cut up for chop suey."

After the taxi had stopped, the Hardys sent Kim-Kim on ahead to reconnoiter the shack. He returned with a big smile. "Nobody home. Okay go see!"

Still somewhat weak-kneed from their narrow escape, Frank, Joe, and Chet tramped across the field until they came to the bone jar. It looked older than the first, and a thin crack ran from the lip to the base.

"You put your hand in this time!" Frank said to Chet.

"Oh no. Not me!"

"I'll do it," Joe volunteered. He reached inside, until his whole arm disappeared. "No bones here," he said, feeling around with his fingers. Finally he pulled out a folded piece of paper. On it was a message. He read it aloud:

" 'Hardys:
Leave the cash here and go a thousand yards up the road. On the opposite side behind a row of trees is an armchair grave. The Ruby King is buried in it. Remember, you are being observed. If you pull any tricks with the money, you will not return to Hong Kong alive!' "

"I expected something like that," Frank said. "We'd better leave the dough."

"But what if the King is not where it's supposed to be?" Joe asked.

"We'll have to take the chance. Put in the money, Joe."

The boy removed the package from his shirt and dropped it into the bone jar. Then they hurried to the taxi and instructed the driver to proceed slowly until they came to the row of eucalyptus trees, about a hundred yards back from the road.

While the driver waited, the four approached the spot. Suddenly voices drifted toward them from behind the trees.

'*Sh!*' Frank warned. "We've got company. Let's sneak up and see who it is!"

Noiselessly they moved to the trees and peered through the branches. There was the armchair grave as the note had indicated, and two men were pulling something out of it. One had his back turned toward the boys, but Frank and Joe recognized the other! He was the man Frank had wrestled with at Ocean Bluffs, just before Gerard Henry and Joe had rolled off the cliff!

Now the other man let out a string of curses and the Hardys recognized his voice.

"It's Reginald Jervis!" Joe whispered.

Frank nodded. "And they're digging up the Ruby King!"

Jervis was still ranting. "Those crooks! Took all the rubies out! It's worthless now, totally worthless!" The men let the King fall down and Jervis kicked it with his foot. "Let's go," he grumbled.

"Oh, no, you don't!" Frank said. The three boys, followed by Kim-Kim, set upon the men like lightning.

Jervis whirled around when he heard the commotion. He still had the shovel in his hand. Instantly he raised it over his head and whacked Joe.

Frank tackled his erstwhile adversary while Chet came to Joe's help. Before Jervis could raise the shovel again, Chet's plaster cast hit him on the side of the head. He toppled and lay still.

Frank, meanwhile, had subdued the other man. "Chet, see if our driver has some rope so we can tie up our buddies," he said.

"I don't think we need it," Chet said. He pointed toward the trees. "Look who's coming!"

Captain Hawkins and another policeman crashed through the branches. "You young foreigners had us worried," he said, "so we tailed Fong's thugs. Followed them to a bone jar and caught them with a bundle of money. You know anything about it?"

While the police snapped handcuffs on the boys' prisoners, Frank and Joe told about the ransom deal.

Jervis laughed out loud. "So Fong was going to let you have the Ruby King after all. But minus the goodies. I thought he'd send you back to

Hong Kong after you had delivered the dough."

"And you figured you could help yourself to the goodies?" Frank asked.

Jervis gritted his teeth. "Fong's a dirty double-crosser! You want him? I'll tell you where he is. Sitting at the Tai Pak Restaurant, waiting for the twenty-five thousand clams!"

"Tai Pak?" Kim-Kim said brightly. "I know. Near where I live. Good place to make money."

Hawkins explained that Tai Pak was a large floating restaurant, famous throughout the Orient. "We'd better go and see if this man is telling the truth," he said.

He ordered the other policeman to take the handcuffed prisoners to headquarters. "I'm going to the waterfront with the boys," he added. "Have a squad car meet me there."

Soon they arrived at the harbor, alive with small canopied boats. They were propelled by women, wearing black pajamas and coolie hats, who sculled the craft along with a long oar.

"Those are water taxis," Hawkins explained. "They take passengers to Tai Pak." He hailed one of the little boats.

The boys noticed that some small open craft were rowed by children. They circled among the fleet of water taxis, begging coins from the more affluent passengers.

"Is that what you meant by a good place to make money?" Chet asked Kim-Kim.

The Chinese nodded and called out to several friends he had recognized.

Just then a squad car arrived with four policemen. While the boys hopped into the water taxi Captain Hawkins had hailed, they took another and soon everyone was headed for the floating restaurant.

The Hardys were amazed at the dexterity of the women, who maneuvered their boats through the traffic without even the slightest collision.

Finally they reached the huge double-deck eating place, colorfully festooned with lights and lanterns. They went aboard and Hawkins suggested that the boys check topside, while the police scoured the main deck.

The Americans were amazed at the size of the restaurant. Scores of tables occupied every foot of the deck. Waiters, carrying large trays, moved through the guests with acrobatic ease.

A broad center staircase led up to the second deck, which was equally crowded.

"Let's split up," Frank suggested. "If you spy Fong, don't make a scene. Just run down and call Captain Hawkins."

The clatter of dishes, the laughter of the diners, and the swiftly moving waiters made concentration difficult. In addition, the savory smell of Chinese cooking made Chet hungry. Nonetheless they spaced out and carefully passed table after table.

Suddenly Joe's eyes fell on Fong. He was seated in a secluded booth next to the wall, talking with another man. Fong glanced nervously at his watch, while his eyes roved the room.

Joe snatched a handkerchief and held it to his face. Then he edged closer, trying to get a look at Fong's companion.

He turned and Joe recognized him. It was the friendly Choy Bok!

A waiter touched Joe's elbow. "Can I help you find a place?"

"No, thank you. Not now."

At that moment Chet hurried to Joe's side. "I see him!" he whispered, and swung his cast in the direction of the booth.

It hit the back of a chair with a sharp crack. The diner sitting there turned around in surprise. At the same time Joe noticed Fong and Choy Bok rise. They had realized that the boys were after them!

"Run down and get the captain!" Joe told Chet. As he hurried off, Frank and Kim-Kim appeared.

"Come on!" Joe cried. "They're getting away!"

The young detectives raced among the tables, trying not to knock into the annoyed patrons.

"There they go! Up the steps!"

The fugitives fairly flew up a small metal stairway onto the roof of the restaurant, and without a moment's hesitation, dived over the railing into the water below.

The Hardys saw them surface and climb into a water taxi.

"After them!" Frank cried out. He and Joe, followed by Kim-Kim, plunged into the bay. They came up next to a surprised taxiwoman and wriggled into her boat. Kim-Kim gave orders in Chinese, and the woman set off after Fong's craft.

"We're losing them!" Joe said. "Faster, please!"

"Don't worry, I help," Kim-Kim said.

He called out to his little beggar friends, who responded with excited cries. Rapidly they began to surround the getaway taxi. With much banging and shouting, they had its path blocked within a few minutes.

It was boxed in so tightly that escape was impossible. The police arrived in another boat with Chet to arrest the two stony-faced fugitives.

Meanwhile, the Hardys emptied their pockets of all their change and tossed the coins to the beggar boys, who grinned and cheered.

"Good job, Kim-Kim," Frank praised the little Chinese.

An hour later everyone met at headquarters. The Hardys were congratulated, and as interrogation of Jervis, Fong, and Choy Bok proceeded, loose ends of the mystery were tied up.

A cablegram from Mr. Hardy had arrived only

minutes before. It said that Eggleby had been caught in the States with Radley's help. He and Jervis had been trying to set up another jewelry operation in Texas, but when Eggleby was caught, Jervis quickly left the country.

Jervis admitted knocking out Mr. Hardy at the Treat Hotel and putting the explosive charge in the boy's tail pipe on orders of Fong. And it was Jervis who shot at Krassner in the balloon fight. Fong and Eggleby were with him at the time.

"You idiot!" Fong muttered. "Why don't you keep your mouth shut?" But the angry gang leader could not do anything to stop his former confederate from telling everything. As he and Choy stood by with suppressed anger, Jervis provided the answer to the serpent gang's interest in Conrad Greene.

"They ran a world-wide gambling operation," Jervis said, "and were trying to frighten the American champion into losing the match because they had placed all bets on his Korean opponent. The phone tap was meant to find out Greene's strategy, and when that did not work, he was kidnapped and threatened."

"Was he taken to Bayport Harbor?" Joe asked.

"No. We drove him to Fong's apartment not far from there."

"Why did you want to ship the Ruby King via

the *Queen Maru?*" Frank inquired. "Is Captain Ono part of your gang?"

"No. He's clean," Jervis said.

"Who went into Krassner's home to steal the King?" Frank asked.

"Fong and Eggleby. They took the antique to the shack in the woods, but when your two buddies arrived, they quickly drove off in Fong's car. Later Gerard Henry had the King wrapped in the rug and took it to Bayport Airport."

"What gave you the idea of using the serpent balloon to harass Krassner?" Joe asked.

"Fong knew Krassner was an avid balloonist," Jervis continued. "He also was well aware that Krassner feared the serpent symbol. The balloon seemed a logical idea to unnerve him."

"But he wouldn't hand over the King, even though you threatened to ruin his reputation," Joe said.

"No. He held out. When we put the pressure on Moy Chen-Chin, Mrs. Krassner cooperated without her husband's knowledge."

"Well, I'm sure glad Krassner is exonerated," Chet said. "I always liked him."

"I'm just sorry we couldn't retrieve the King undamaged," Joe put in. "Without its jewels the chess piece is probably worthless."

"Fong knows where the rubies are. Ask him!" Jervis said.

"I know nothing," the Oriental said as his face contorted in an arrogant sneer.

"Where does Fong live?" Frank asked Jervis.

The man shrugged. "He's been staying with Choy Bok ever since he arrived."

"Why don't we look in Choy's apartment?" Joe suggested. "We know where it is!"

"Good idea," Captain Hawkins said.

An hour later a search party with a warrant arrived at Choy's high-rise apartment. There was no sign of Mrs. Choy. The police combed the place until one of them yelled, "Captain, come here!" In the pocket of Mrs. Choy's dressing gown was a sack of gems!

Captain Hawkins invited the boys and Kim-Kim to dinner that night and thanked them for smashing the serpent gang. "Please return the Ruby King to its rightful owner," he said. "It won't be hard to restore it to its original beauty."

"You go back to United States?" Kim-Kim asked, his eyes sad.

"We'll have to. The case is solved," Joe said. Little did he know then that soon they would be involved in another one, *The Mysterious Caravan*.

Chet put an arm around his little friend. "We must leave. But we have a surprise for you. Frank and Joe have decided that part of their fee rightfully belongs to you because of your help!"

Kim-Kim's eyes lit up. "Me good detective!"

"A friend of ours," Chet went on, "will come to Hong Kong soon for the big chess championship. His name is Conrad Greene. He'll give you your reward. You just tell Captain Hawkins where he can get in touch with you."

"Speaking about the chess match," Joe said, "now that all the pressure is off, Conrad might win it, and with it the Ruby King!"

"And old Mr. Greene won't have to worry any more," Frank added with a smile. "The King was buried not by its owner, but by Fong's men. The curse is lifted!"

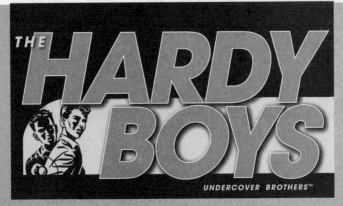

# Match Wits with The Hardy Boys®!

## Collect the Complete
## Hardy Boys Mystery Stories®
by Franklin W. Dixon

**Celebrate over 70 Years with the World's Greatest Super Sleuth**